The Ghosts Who Waited

"Fat chance," muttered William as he pumped up his airbed. "I hate this place. I always will. It – it…" he was searching for what he wanted to say… "It doesn't like me."

"You mean you don't like *it*, surely?" said Rosy.

"No." William turned to her and shouted. "*It* doesn't like *me*. Can't you feel it? It doesn't like any of us."

"I'm frightened," said Louise again, in a small voice.

"I don't think it wants us to be here," said William.

HIPPO GHOST

The Ghosts Who Waited

Dennis Hamley

Hippo

Scholastic Children's Books
Commonwealth House, 1–19 New Oxford Street,
London WC1A 1NU, UK
a division of Scholastic Ltd
London ~ New York ~ Toronto ~ Sydney ~ Auckland

First published by Scholastic Ltd, 1997

Text copyright © Dennis Hamley, 1997

ISBN 0 590 19367 8

Typeset by TW Typesetting, Midsomer Norton, Somerset
Printed by Cox & Wyman Ltd, Reading, Berks.

10 9 8 7 6 5 4 3 2 1

For James and Rebecca

Prologue

*H*ow can you tell when a house is haunted? Perhaps it's just a feeling – all is not quite right in it. Perhaps there's more. There may be voices in the air which you can't quite hear, or shadows which seem to move when they shouldn't.

Perhaps only a very few visitors ever know more than that – but then, they may have a right to.

Let's see what went on in Dyson's Cottage.

The old house had been empty for a long time. Behind it were dark, mysterious woods which, after sunset, were full of the sounds of night creatures. To the front were wide fields where cattle grazed. A rough cart track stretched from the cottage's broken-down front gate to the road and the little town a mile beyond.

Wind whistled through cracked window panes and found holes in broken roof slates. The wind was followed by rain searching out cracks and crevices, leaving a damp, musty smell nobody sniffed any more. There were some who said that more than just wind moaned through the house and the night creatures did not roam alone when the sun was down.

Others scoffed. "What's in the past is gone for ever," they said. But was that true for this old house? Unquiet, invisible spirits coursed up and down the bare staircase. They lingered on the stone floor in the cold scullery. They hovered round the unkempt garden where once vegetables grew and baskets of blackcurrants and gooseberries were picked in the trim shrubbery. Nobody ever heard their long, never-ending conversation. Over the years, though, many had tried to live in the house and found these spirits there. They had felt presences in bedrooms, sensed companions at mealtimes. They knew the talking went on. They heard rustling that no mouse made, low flutings that came from no bird's throat. Sometimes there was whispering which made them think of great anger, cruelty which made them shudder. Sometimes in the patter of the rain there was faint crying as if of deep misery beyond anything they could imagine.

People who had come with such hope to live in the cottage and make it whole again always left soon after. They mumbled to folk in the town about lonely country life not suiting them after all. And, just beyond their hearing, the conversation had gone on and on...

"When will they see me? When can I tell them?"

"Never. No one will know what happened here. The secrets of this place will stay secret."

"But they mustn't stay secret. How can they? Evil must always be found out."

"Forget your Sunday School lessons. You'll see nobody and tell nobody because nobody cares."

"They will. They must."

"Nobody cared about you then. Nobody ever cared about anyone here. That was how it was. That is how it always will be."

"No. Someone will come who cares. There has to be."

"Nobody."

"*Then I will wait. There is a debt to pay, amends to make.*"

"Nobody."

"*That is wrong. One day the person will come who can hear my message. Then I will walk abroad again.*"

"Never. Nobody."

"*I wait. The day will come…*"

Round and round the house the spirits wandered and the voices called. But in all that time, no one came who could see them or make out their words. The gentle voice of hope grew fainter, the deep and cruel voice grew louder – as once, long ago, they had in the world of people, places and things.

Chapter 1

Miles away, in a road of new houses, Rosy, William and Louise were happy. They liked their friends, their schools, the town they lived in.

But they knew that all was not well...

Dad worked for an engineering firm on a big industrial estate. Everybody knew things were not right there – orders going down, no more overtime, short-time working, rumours that this couldn't continue, that there would be a takeover or even a shutdown. It was all the talk at school – many of Rosy's, William's and Louise's friends also had parents who worked there. Gloom enwrapped everybody.

Except, it seemed, Mum and Dad. Rosy, the oldest, kept wondering whether she should ask why Mum and Dad seemed almost to grow happier as the news from the factory became more dire. On at least two occasions, the children knew, Dad had taken a day off when they were at school.

"Isn't that a silly thing to do when he may be going to get the sack?" said William. "They might think he doesn't *want* to work there."

That's right, thought Rosy. Then she said something that had been on her mind for some time. "Do you know? I don't think he does want to work there any more."

William and Louise were sure Rosy was right. There was the air around the place of a secret being kept that the children were not allowed in on. They felt resentful.

"What do they do on these days off?" asked Louise.

"They go away," said William.

"Where to?" said Rosy.

None of them knew. Once, though, when Dad had been off and it had been raining,

William had come home from school and noticed the car's body was flecked with mud and the tyre walls were thick with it.

"They've driven down dirt tracks," he said. "Like they'd been camping on a farm."

Next day, the green Vauxhall was shining again. The evidence had been hosed off.

"Why don't we just ask?" said Louise.

Rosy immediately felt that would be wrong. There would be enough for them all to worry about later. Why shouldn't Mum and Dad go off for a quick day on their own? They deserved to be private now and again.

The next day, everything became clear.

School was over, supper was beginning. They were all sitting round the table.

Dad cleared his throat. "We've got two things to tell you," he said.

They waited expectantly.

"First, I've been made redundant," he said.

"What's that?" said Louise.

"The firm, they say, is downsizing."

Rosy knew at once what that meant. Not quite as cosy as it sounded.

"And they're letting me go," Dad continued.

Rosy had a sudden vision of Dad held fast by the leg in a cruel mantrap and gentle hands releasing him so he could run joyfully into the sunshine.

"Does that mean you've got the sack?" said William.

"Yes," said Dad.

There was silence. This is dreadful, Rosy thought. What are we going to do?

More to the point, why were Mum and Dad sitting at opposite ends of the table with broad smiles on their faces?

"It happens to everybody," said Dad. "Nowadays, if you haven't been made redundant, you haven't lived."

"But it's a *disaster*..." Rosy started.

"It could be a lot worse," said Mum. "They're at least paying Dad some redundancy money. Not a huge amount, but enough for what we want."

"If they weren't," said Dad, "we couldn't tell you the second thing."

There was *more*? Wasn't that shock enough

for one day?

"You may not like this," said Dad.

"We're all leaving here," said Mum.

Silence. Dad was right. First thoughts were that they didn't like it.

"But all my friends are here," wailed Louise.

William said nothing. His mouth turned down angrily.

Rosy too felt sudden anger. She had only started secondary school that year. It was all right for the others. They would be changing schools soon anyway. After three terms she had got used to her new school. Would she have to grapple with a third in as many years? And with strangers? Her heart sank at the prospect.

"It will be all right," said Dad. But his voice was not as confident as it had been a few minutes before.

"Where are we supposed to be going to?" said William. His voice was sullen.

"We've seen an old place in the country," said Mum.

The children exchanged glances. Of course: the days away, the mud on the car. But all this without consulting them? Resentment filled the air even more strongly.

"But you haven't got it yet," said Rosy hopefully.

"We're buying it with the redundancy money," said Dad. "It's dirt cheap because there's so much needs doing to it and it's miles away from anywhere. I think the estate agent was thankful to get it off his hands."

Worse and worse.

"We're selling this house and camping in the other one while we do it up. We can live cheaply, grow our own food and look for jobs in the new place."

Silence. Then: "It sounds horrible," said William. "I don't want to go."

Rosy and Louise said nothing. But they agreed with William.

"I'm afraid there's no choice," said Dad. "I won't get another job in this town. Your mother could get some part-time work but we'd never live off it and I can't sit at home all day. If I don't get some good paying work we won't be able to keep up the payments on the house. It will be repossessed and we'll be out on the streets. This way, we'll have a choice and *we're doing something for ourselves.* Now, which do you want?"

There was no answer. He was right, of course. But it came hard.

"Where is this place?" asked Rosy.

"About forty miles away," Mum answered. "Near a lovely old place called Great Marston. The house has got a name. It's Dyson's Cottage."

"Pity Dyson didn't stay in it," William muttered.

Mum looked at him sharply. "We're all in this together, William," she said. "Your father didn't ask to lose his job."

"Wait till you see the cottage," said Dad. "You might change your tune."

Rosy looked at the others. Louise, head down, was staring at her half-empty plate. Even as Rosy watched, she pushed it away. William still looked rebellious. But he made no answer to Dad. Instead, he chomped mechanically through his food, as if the chicken pieces, cauliflower and baked potato were prison rations.

Chapter 2

William was nearly ten. He was stocky, with fair hair. Everybody said he took after Mum. Rosy lay in bed that night thinking about him. She knew he would find leaving very difficult: his friends, his football, his swapping of computer games – everything he wanted was here and not in some field in the back of beyond.

Louise was seven, with light brown hair and grey eyes. Just like Dad's. Rosy knew, once the surprise was over, that she wouldn't take it as hard as William – though how she would get on while the rest were helping Dad with any heavy work she wasn't quite sure. Louise's big crisis may come later, she thought.

And *was* this wish for the simple life such a good idea after all? Rosy knew well that it was born of desperation. Mum and Dad had seen the writing on the wall. And Rosy had worked out for herself that a bad time was coming even before Dad's announcement. She had enough friends at school whose families were in trouble. But was this the way to sort it out? How much of a ruin was Dyson's Cottage?

Dad was good at DIY. Anything in the house, he could do. No builder needed to come to fix the roof when the tiles blew off in the gales. No plumber had ever crossed the threshold. Electrical jobs were no trouble. But was that the same as rebuilding on his own – with whatever puny help the four of them could give – a place which she had a shrewd suspicion might prove to be a ruin? No builders would be called in – Rosy knew they couldn't afford them. What sort of back-breaking trial were they all in for?

Unlike William and Louise, Rosy's worries as she waited for sleep were not about what she would leave behind, but what she would find when she got there.

Rosy was twelve. She was tall, with very dark hair and eyes that were nearly black. She looked quite different from all the others. Why? Because she was adopted. She had known this for as long as she could remember, though the day she had been told was now long forgotten. Mum and Dad had been married for seven years with no sign of a child. So they had gone to an adoption agency and the arrival of three-month-old Rosy had been the result. Rosy did not know who her real parents were. One day, she had resolved the previous year, she would find out.

Meanwhile, though, Rosy had found parents: they had found a daughter. Yet – so often it happens – no sooner was Rosy saying her first words, beginning to walk, looked on as a natural part of the family, than a child of their own was on its way for Mum and Dad. First came William, then Louise. Two real, one adopted. But never was Rosy loved any less, never was she anything but the eldest child in the family.

Just as well, she thought before sleep finally

overtook her. Those two are going to need some careful handling.

They could not move for another two months. Dad had to finish his time with the firm and the redundancy money would not be paid out until then. Also, even though nobody had lived in Dyson's Cottage for years now, the solicitors took all that time to finish the legal work. Besides, they had to find a buyer for their own house. Mum and Dad feared this would be the hardest job of all – but they were lucky. A family turned up almost at once, liked what they saw and were willing to pay the asking price. So all was set for the end of July, two days after the school summer holidays started.

The day of moving would be the first time the children would see Dyson's Cottage. William and Louise never asked to go: Rosy murmured to Mum that it would not be a good idea.

"It's going to be hard for them to leave their friends," she said. "Going there before they have to will make it even worse for them."

"You're right, Rosy," Mum had replied. "Sensible as always. Anyway, between you and me, if they saw the place as it is now, before they have to, we'd *never* get them to shift on the day."

What Mum had meant as thanks for a good piece of advice kept Rosy awake at night with worry.

The removal van did not follow them to Dyson's Cottage. The furniture was to be put in store. Later on, they would bring what they wanted when the house was ready and sell the rest. Everything they needed for now – airbeds, sleeping bags, Calor Gas cylinders with a heater, lamps and a stove from camping holidays – was crammed into the trailer hitched up to the back of the Vauxhall.

Dad started the engine: they moved away. Rosy saw, as the house she had lived in for all her remembered life grew smaller behind them, that Louise's face was running with tears and William was fighting against tears of his own.

The journey was silent. Nobody said, though they could have done, "What a lovely place!" as they slipped through the wide High Street of Great Marston with its old buildings either side. Nobody commented as Dad stopped at the estate agents to pick up the keys to Dyson's Cottage. As the car, a mile out of the town, headed off the main road down a narrow lane, the atmosphere was tense. Dad stopped the car. Mum got out and opened a five-barred gate. Then Dad turned the car off the lane, Mum closed the gate and climbed in again. The car and trailor bumped along a rutted cart-track across a field which seemed vast like a small prairie and the atmosphere descended to something awful beyond description.

The car climbed up a shallow rise and breasted the near horizon. There, in front of them, was a line of dark trees: the edge of a forest.

"Marston Woods," said Dad as they approached. "They stretch for miles. There's a lake in the middle, I'm told. Marston Mere."

Those were the first words spoken inside the car since leaving the old house.

The cart-track was nearing its end.

"There's Dyson's Cottage," said Dad.

They stared at the little house, square, built of brick, with a front door in the middle and two downstairs windows, one each side, small, with many little panes. Upstairs were two windows exactly the same. As they drew closer they could see some panes were broken; one window at least was hanging open; the mortar between the bricks was crumbling. Straggly briars fell across the door. The roof had tiles missing and a chimney pot was cracked. Behind the broken garden fence, long grass waved and out-of-control bushes writhed at one end.

The sun had gone in: the air struck cold as Mum and Dad got out and opened the car doors. The sudden chill seemed a fitting welcome. The silence intensified.

Then: "What a dump," William said disgustedly.

Louise's face screwed up. She was crying again.

Mum and Dad looked at each other help-lessly. "It will be lovely one day," said Mum weakly. "We all have to work together."

"There's nothing we can't tackle if we put our minds to it," said Dad.

"What do you think of it, Rosy?" said Mum.

Instead of answering, Rosy said, "What's that?" She was pointing to a stone set above the door, carved with letters. *G.D. 1880.*

"The initials of the man who had it built," said Dad. "And the date."

"D for Dyson," said Mum.

"What's G for?" said William. "Gary?"

"Not in 1880," said Mum.

Rosy listened to these answers but said nothing. She was staring at the door, the windows each side, the other windows above looking like half-blind eyes – as if the front wall of Dyson's Cottage was a face whose expression she needed to read.

Yes, this is where we had to come, she wanted to say. *This is my place, this was meant for me.*

But how could she? They would ask what she meant and she wouldn't have a clue. She shook her head to free herself of such fancies.

"You're right," she said. "We could make it lovely."

Louise suddenly grasped Mum's hand. "Mummy," she said. "I'm frightened."

Chapter 3

Dad turned the key in the lock. The door swung open into a dark passageway with doors leading off either side and a scullery beyond. Scraps of old wallpaper, once flowery but now brown, stuck to – and sometimes waved from – the walls. William switched on an old brown Bakelite light switch: nothing happened.

"No power yet," said Dad.

Now they were all aware of a strong, musty smell. Gloom descended even further.

"Have we *got* to live here?" William muttered.

"It's not as bad as it looks," said Dad. His breeziness, thought Rosy, sounded forced. "It just needs warming up, drying through and the holes in the roof sealed up."

William started to walk upstairs. Dad stopped him.

"Not yet," he said. "The staircase may be rotten. I'll have to give it a good going over before anybody goes up there. For now we'll camp on the ground floor."

William stared upstairs as if the Holy Grail was overhead. For a moment Rosy thought he might run up there anyway, and had visions of the staircase collapsing under his weight or a leg getting trapped as one step rotted suddenly beneath him. *Don't even think about it*, she willed him in thought. *Things are bad enough*.

"Let's unpack the car and trailer," Mum said quickly. "Then we can have light, warmth and something to eat."

"I'll need some of my tools," said Dad. "Especially the hammer."

Unwillingly, William turned away from the stairs.

They had only been in the house a few minutes, yet going outside seemed like being let out of prison. For a few brief moments everything was forgotten as sleeping bags, airbeds, folding chairs and table, torches, two Tilley lamps and a camping stove were ferried in. Just for that instant it seemed as though they were starting another camping holiday. Dad lugged in his big metal toolbox.

"The water should be on," he said. "I asked the Water Company to make sure. I've just got to turn it on at the mains."

After a few minutes' search at the back of the scullery he found the mains tap. There was a gurgle from the pipes: then he tried to turn the single tap over the stone sink in the scullery. It wouldn't move. He took his hammer and whacked it: then turned again. It shifted with difficulty and a thin trickle of brown water dribbled out.

"Yuk," said Louise, watching.

"It will get better," said Dad, and he turned the tap further. Suddenly, clear water foamed out.

"There," said Dad triumphantly. "Doesn't that make you feel better?"

Not a lot, obviously, thought Rosy, looking round.

"Can you turn the electricity on now?" said William.

"No electricity yet, I'm afraid," said Dad. "The wiring's rotten. I'm going to rewire the house myself. Proper circuit breakers, everything up to the minute, no more dreadful old death-trap fuseboxes. But you'll have to wait a bit for that."

"No television?" wailed Louise.

"What about my computer?" demanded William.

"We told you that before," said Mum.

"As soon as I can, I promise," said Dad.

Louise didn't answer. The dreadful news could not have sunk in at the time.

"We've got a transistor radio," said Dad. "And it won't be for long. Besides, Louise, haven't you got your tapes and cassette player?"

The camping stove was set up, a kettle boiled. Mugs of tea and a makeshift meal were made. Very slightly, spirits rose.

Rosy sat next to Louise and remembered her words before they came in. She spoke softly in Louise's ear.

"You're not frightened now, are you?"

"I think I'll always be frightened here."

Rosy straightened up. *I'm not frightened*, she thought. *Because this is my place that we've come to.*

That strong feeling again. Why? What did it mean?

Beyond the scullery at the back was a dank and tiny bathroom and loo into which, the moment she saw it, Louise insisted she would never go. The passage from the front door to the scullery had two doors leading from it, one either side, directly opposite each other. Behind each door was a square room with a small front window. The rooms were exactly the same in size and the identical windows would not let much light in through their many tiny panes. Rosy wondered if one room had been meant as a dining room, the other as a sitting room.

"Are the rooms the same upstairs?" she asked Dad.

"No," was the answer. "The stairs lead to a landing going across the back of the house. There are two main bedrooms looking out of the front windows and a very tiny third room, hardly more than a big cupboard, off the landing at the back and over the scullery." He saw her face fall as she did the quick mental calculation which told her that even when all the work was finished she would still be sharing a room.

"I've got plans to divide one of the front bedrooms in two. A proper dividing wall and an extra door should do it. And a new window at the side. One day I want to replace all the windows with larger ones."

"So where are we going to sleep now?" demanded William.

"Your mother and I in the room to the right. You three can set up your airbeds in the other."

Outside, dusk was approaching. Nobody wanted to explore beyond the doors, to brave the dark and overgrown garden. The presence just beyond the fence of Marston Woods oppressed them – miles of gnarled trunks, twisted branches and brambly paths to nowhere, teeming with unknown life, and far away at its heart the dark, silent waters of a lake. Mum lit the two Tilley lamps.

"We may as well get ready for bed," she said. "We've got to start work early tomorrow to begin to make this place habitable."

The children lugged airbeds and sleeping bags into the room Dad had assigned them. On their own, the atmosphere was even more gloomy. The stone floor was cold to their feet. Rosy guessed that in the other room Mum and Dad would be looking at each other without a word, but their faces would be saying, "Have we done the right thing?"

"It will be all right in the end," Rosy said as if answering their question.

"Fat chance," muttered William as he pumped up his airbed. "I hate this place. I always will. It – it…" he was searching for what he wanted to say… "It doesn't like me."

"You mean you don't like *it*, surely?" said Rosy.

"No." William turned to her and shouted. "*It* doesn't like *me*. Can't you feel it? It doesn't like any of us."

"I'm frightened," said Louise again, in a small voice.

"I don't think it wants us to be here," said William.

"I don't know what you mean," said Rosy.

"I saw it as soon as we got here. The front of the house is like a face, a really *stupid* face."

So he saw it too, thought Rosy.

"And do you know what it was saying? 'Go away.' I wish we had. Now we're inside, I feel as if I'm not supposed to go in any room. They're not for me. They want me to stay out. That's why I won't. That's why I wanted to go upstairs. They won't stop me."

Rosy knew that by "they" he didn't just mean Mum and Dad.

"Don't you feel it?" said William.

"You only feel like this because the house is all broken down and damp and you didn't want to leave home," said Rosy.

"No. There's something else." He stopped for a moment. Then he spoke again, his tone different. "Look, I know why Mum and Dad had to leave the old place. I'm not daft. I don't like it but I know it had to happen. Now we're here I should really want to help. I should be looking round and thinking how great it's going to be when it's all done. But I can't. Because *the house won't let me.*"

He had finished pumping his airbed. He spread out his sleeping bag on it.

Rosy was on the point of saying, "It's different for me." But she checked herself. For her to tell William that she had felt the opposite – *this is where we have to be; this is my place* – would only start a row. And that was the last thing they wanted now.

Chapter 4

Rosy had been given charge of the Tilley lamp. It hissed and cast its soft yellow light from just an arm's length away from her head. She lay for a long time watching it. She could see the others stretched out on their sleeping bags. Nobody seemed to want to talk tonight. This was very unlike the first night of a holiday, other times when they had been stretched out in their sleeping bags by the light of a Tilley lamp. But then they had been in a tent, other tents had companionably stretched away from them on either side: there were friends to make, warm seas close by, all the joys of holiday to look forward to. Here, the next day would bring hard work and an unknown future. It seemed almost a betrayal of the sleeping bags and all they were supposed to stand for.

Louise had closed her eyes straight away. Rosy doubted if she were asleep. William was trying to read, augmenting the Tilley lamp's light with his torch. She saw his brow wrinkled and his eyes screwed up in the bad light and knew without his having to say so that he was resentfully remembering his room at home all to himself, his reading lamp, his posters, his computer...

Moths and smaller insects fluttered round the warm element of the lamp. Their wings glowed luminously. Beyond, shadows seemed to flit across the room in the light, slight darkenings, stainings, of the yellow. There were draughts in here: the room was cold: cold even seemed to filter up through the airbed into the sleeping bag from the stone floor. Rosy watched the shadows. She drowsily supposed the draughts would some-how be bending the lamp's warm glow as a breeze would alter the direction of flames. She heard noises: rustlings, cracklings, chirrupings, the soft moan of wind. The house seemed alive, like a sleeping animal. The old, long-deserted structure must now be home to thousands of creatures – mice, bats, birds. Rats? She shuddered. No. There was no food here, nothing to attract them. They were too far away from other houses. Perhaps loneliness had one or two advantages.

Even so, she drew the sleeping bag up further round her head. There was sound, movement, all round her. What would it be like when the light was off?

A disturbing idea flashed unbidden into her mind. *Of course a draught would not alter the direction of light. Nothing could. The steady light from the Tilley lamp should remain constant.* She strained her eyes to follow those slight darkenings of light the shadows made, and into her mind came the strange fancy that they were not shadows at all but presences.

Don't be silly, Rosy. She looked at her watch. It was time. Besides, she shouldn't let the lamp burn too long: it would run out of gas and they didn't know yet where to get refills from.

"I'm turning the lamp off," she said.

By now, Louise really was asleep. William answered, "I'm going on reading with my torch on."

"Don't wake Louise with it," said Rosy.

In the new darkness, Rosy found the little glow from William's torch very comforting. But even that didn't last long. He must have been as worried about his batteries as Rosy was about the gas cylinder.

After he switched it off and said, "Good night, Rosy," the darkness seemed to settle on them like an extra blanket. The house noises seemed suddenly louder, as if it had turned up its volume control.

After a few minutes, William said, "I don't like this. It feels like there's things walking all over the floor."

"It's nothing. It just seems like that," Rosy replied.

William didn't answer. But a few minutes afterwards he flashed his torch on again.

"Who's got out of bed?" he said. "It's a bit soon to be going to the loo."

"Nobody's out of bed," said Rosy.

"But I was sure that..." He flashed his torch all round, saw Rosy unmoving, Louise asleep. "Well, that's very funny."

"Calm down, William," said Rosy. "There's nothing. It's just an old, strange place and we have to get used to it."

William switched his torch off. A few minutes later his deep breathing told Rosy that in spite of everything he was asleep. She lay awake a long time before sleep came to her. She couldn't get out of her mind the nagging ideas, first, that this wasn't *just* an old, strange place and, second, that it was going to take a very great deal of getting used to.

Usually, the light of day blew away all memories of a bad night. But this was not so when Rosy, William and Louise, woken up by the radio in the scullery belting out Radio 1, emerged to breakfast. This consisted of toast laboriously made on the grill of the camping stove, plus cereals and coffee made with longlife milk.

"No fresh until we've got power and can get the fridge on," said Mum.

The refrigerator, like the electric oven, television and all the other furniture, would not come out of store until the house was fit to receive them.

"Did you sleep well?" asked Mum brightly. They looked at each other. They had certainly slept long. But it had not been good sleep. All three knew they had had weird, disturbing dreams which had vanished the moment their eyes had opened to the light through the small window. Vanished though the dreams may have been, the disturbance stayed on in their minds and they were subdued and quiet. But there was an unspoken agreement – they wouldn't tell their parents. This was not the time to go upsetting them.

"We must go into Great Marston today," said Dad. "You can all find a supermarket while I look for a tool hire centre and a builders' merchant. I need a scaling ladder to get right up on the roof. I've got to replace all those missing slates. And there's glass and putty for the windows needed. I want the place at least weathertight and draughtproof by tonight."

They took turns in washing sketchily at the stone sink with a kettleful of hot water each.

"Does this mean cold baths?" asked Louise, dismayed.

"Lukewarm at best for a while, I fear," said Mum.

"I'll be fitting a proper hot-water heater when I've done the wiring," said Dad. "And an electric shower as well. One day there'll be central heating from a log stove and then a proper boiler with lashings of hot water all the time. Remember, there's no gas this far out of town."

The prospect Dad painted seemed like a mirage on the far horizon.

After breakfast, they made a first exploration of the garden. Even hazy sunshine could not make it look beautiful. The grass needed scything, not mowing. Weeds were thick in it. At the far end, the shrubbery was impenetrable. Daunted by the work ahead, they came back to the house.

Immediately outside the scullery was a backyard paved with stones, most of which were lifted up by weeds underneath. Opposite the scullery was a line of outhouses. One with inside walls still black was obviously once a coalhouse. Next to it was a foul-smelling, though long disused, outside loo which made Louise think even the one indoors was preferable. The third had walls which still showed they were whitewashed.

"A wash-house," said Mum. "There would be a big tub to stir the clothes in, a copper to boil the water and a mangle to wring them through. Someone once had to work *very* hard in here."

In the coalhouse, Dad made a discovery. A neat stack of slates, left as if ready to do the job he had planned for today.

"That's good," he said. "Saves me buying. And slates aren't easy to come by nowadays." He thought for a moment. "Whoever's lived here before did quite a lot of work before they left. Someone put that bathroom and loo indoors. It's ancient stuff: it must have been done a few years ago. And someone was going to do the roof. Funny nobody ever seemed to stay long enough to make a proper job of them."

"I bet I know why," said William.

Mum looked at him questioningly. Before he could go any further, Rosy quickly said, "Come on. Let's see what the town has to offer."

There were some topics that should not be dwelt on too much for a while.

William said no more. But as soon as they were in the car and it was bumping along the cart-track, he muttered to Rosy, "I don't care what Dad says. I'm going up those stairs as soon as I can."

Chapter 5

Spirits lifted slightly as they bumped their way down the cart-track and out into the lane. The sun shone. Though the field between Dyson's Cottage and the gate was vast, like a bare Russian steppe, the result of a farmer's wish for uninterrupted land to cultivate, there were still high hedges by the grass verges of the lane outside. Tall chestnut trees arched overhead and made a comforting tunnel, broken by a tracery of sunbeams shining through the branches as they drove along. Once on the main road, they felt like returning explorers approaching the base camp.

As they dropped down the hill into Great Marston they passed an industrial estate. "I bet there's a builders' merchants in there," said William.

"Good thinking," said Dad, and he turned in. William was right.

"OK," said Dad. "I'll drop you all in town, come back here, stock up, look for a tool hire place and then meet you in two hours at the place where I leave you."

It was agreed. Five minutes later Dad was gone and the others stood looking round them in the bustling High Street. Dyson's Cottage and the dark night seemed part of another existence.

They found a supermarket, stocked up with provisions for a week, wondered how to carry eight full plastic bags easily, then bought a large basket and a shopping trolley.

"I never had this trouble at home," said Mum.

"It's not home now," William said sharply.

William feels as though this morning's like a prisoner's parole, thought Rosy.

In a sort of way, so did she. But while William had expressed unrelieved fear and loathing of the cottage, she could not get rid of that first feeling that, however ghastly a place it was, it was *hers*, that she was meant to be there. *What am I, if where I'm meant to be is a place the others hate?* she thought.

No. Let worries like that drop away while you've got a chance to forget them for an hour or two.

"Let's explore the town," she said. "It looks nice."

So they did. It was. The High Street dropped into a valley and rose again the other side. Antique shops vied with modern stores with hardly one empty, boarded up, for sale or to let: there was a feeling that here everything was solid, prosperous and confident. Different from the town they had left.

They entered a small café, sat at a table surrounded by chattering people and drank coffee. Louise had a Pepsi.

"I'd love to feel part of this place," said Rosy suddenly.

"But we're not, are we," William answered. "We're broke and hopeless, living in a hovel."

"*William!*" cried Mum. "How dare you say that?"

"But it's true, isn't it? We'll never be part of it. We'll never be part of anything again."

Mum didn't answer. Suddenly the coffee was cold and bitter.

"We'd better be out and waiting for your father," Mum said.

He was there dead on time. The trailer was loaded and covered: a hired scaling ladder, with its curled end to fit over the ridge tiles at the top of the roof, was strapped down on top. He sat silent and unsmiling as they loaded the shopping into the boot. Then he drove away without a word. Silence settled oppressively in the car.

"What's the matter, Daddy?" said Louise as they passed the last houses and were on the main road.

"Nothing, Louise," Dad replied.

"Yes, there is," said Mum quietly.

Dad looked straight ahead for a moment. Finally, unwillingly, he spoke.

"Well, if you must know, it's what everybody in the builders' merchants said when they found out where we were living. They all know Dyson's Cottage. They think we're mad to go there. They say it's not worth even trying to do up. It should be left to rot. If anybody did work on it, they'd need a mint of money and a whole building firm to gut the place and make a proper job of it. They all say it's beyond one person to do."

"You've got us," said Rosy quietly.

"They're wrong, aren't they, love?" said Mum. "We can do it, can't we?"

"I told them so. I got quite angry. Do you know what one of them said?"

"No, Dad. We weren't there," said William sarcastically.

Mum turned round from the front seat and shot him a furious glare. "I've about had enough of you for one day," she hissed.

" 'On your own heads be it.' That's what he said. 'On your own heads be it. That place should be blown up, not rebuilt.' I asked him what he meant. 'You'll find out,' he said."

Nobody spoke again. Mum got out and opened the gate to the track: the car banged up the slope, breasted the horizon – and there was Dyson's Cottage, its brick frontage with the too-symmetrical features: front door with *G.D. 1880* carved over it, small windows, all combining into that sullen, unwelcoming face staring at them and willing them to pass straight by.

But of course they didn't pass by. Soon they were outside and unloading. William helped Dad unstrap the scaling ladder and sort out and stack up the building materials he had bought.

"Come on, Rosy and Louise," Mum said with forced cheerfulness. "You two and I can make a nice ham salad with boiled new potatoes for lunch."

"Mum," said Rosy as she washed the lettuce. "That was awful, what they said to Dad."

"Take no notice. They don't know what they're talking about."

"But what happens if the place is just too much for us to do?"

Mum turned to face her. Rosy was suddenly shocked to notice for the first time that over the last few days she seemed to have aged ten years. "Don't say such things. We *have* to do it. We've burned our boats. There's nothing else for us."

Rosy said nothing, but got on with the lettuce.

Dad and William came in for their lunch. It was obvious they hadn't spoken much. Dad ate for a while, then said, "I'll be up on the roof this afternoon. It shouldn't need more than a few new tiles. There's only trouble if the lead flashing round the chimney's gone. I'll need someone to stay at the bottom of the extending ladder on the ground and pass up the tiles to me."

"All afternoon?" said William. His face showed how appalling he found the prospect.

"Take it in turns," said Dad. "But there's no just standing there and dreaming. If the ladder on the ground slips and pulls the scaling ladder away from the roof, I'm dead."

"I'll go round the back," said Mum. "It's a lovely day: we've got to be outside. We'll start by getting rid of some of those weeds in the backyard."

They really are trying to rally everyone round, thought Rosy. She looked at William's face. He was boiling up to say something. Rosy wondered what, in his present mood, it might be.

She soon knew. "This house doesn't like us," he said. "Be careful on the roof, Dad. It might *try* to throw you off."

Chapter 6

The afternoon was bright and warm. Being outside should have been a real pleasure. But the same thought was running through the minds of Rosy, William and Louise. *This is not how we should be spending a lovely day in summer. We should be by a beach and our meal should have been outside a tent on a camping site in Cornwall or France.*

Rosy was the first to stand at the bottom rung of the ladder. She helped Dad extend the big aluminium ladder against the wall, then waited until he was nearly at the top before she passed up the scaling ladder. He pushed it up in front of him and across the slates until it hooked over the ridge tiles at the top of the roof. Then, standing on his big ladder, he gave the scaling ladder a strong pull.

"It stayed where it should. Thank heavens for that," he said. "The ridge tiles are strong, that's something."

He had placed the scaling ladder next to the chimney. Now he climbed up, gingerly picking his way over the slates, his toes just balancing on the rungs of the scaling ladder, until he could carefully examine the lead flashing round the chimney.

"There's nothing wrong with it," he called down. "It all seems watertight."

He came down.

"The flashing's OK, the ridge tiles are firm – this house isn't nearly so bad as those chaps at the builders' merchants made out. *Someone's* done some work on it and not too long ago, either."

"Is it safe up there?" asked Rosy anxiously.

"Of course it is. Safe as houses. That William talks a load of rubbish. *This house doesn't like us,* indeed. Where does he get his ideas from? Get ready to pass me up some slates, Rosy."

Now came a long period while Dad looked for broken slates, took them out, brought them down, took up the new slates Rosy gave him and fixed them in place over the joists. Dad went methodically up and down, every so often shifting the ladders further along the front of the house. Rosy was never bored: she was watchful and ready, always having enough of the heavy slates ready for him, always making sure the extending ladder was firm on the ground while he was on it, watching anxiously as he clung on to the scaling ladder and lay flat on the roof as he replaced the slates. She had watched houses being reroofed by proper builders. They seemed to think nothing of *walking* across steeply-pitched roofs, sure in their balance. Dad might be a good handyman, but he was just an amateur and more than once Rosy wondered if the people at the builders' merchants weren't right and this was all too much for them.

And if William's outburst at lunch was right ... but if the house didn't like them, it must for the afternoon have called a truce. Dad seemed very happy.

"Slow but sure, eh?" he said when he had replaced sixteen slates. "Now I'm used to being up there I'm rather enjoying this."

A voice sounded behind Rosy. "My turn here," said Mum.

In the backyard, things were rather different.

"This is *boring*," said Louise.

They were scraping with trowels between each paving stone to gouge out the weeds which grew in the cracks. To Rosy, they didn't seem to have done very much.

"By rights, we should dig the stones up," she said. "We'll never get down to the roots if we don't."

William looked disgusted. "Do me a favour," he said.

They carried on. Rosy tried to hurry them up: even so, it was some time before all the cracks were clear of the unwanted greenery. By now Dad had finished at the front and the ladders were being set up at the back.

Mum watched the three in the yard.

"My turn on the ladders again?" asked Rosy hopefully.

"You've done a great job here," said Mum, admiringly but, Rosy suspected, not altogether truthfully. "See what you can do in the garden. Besides, it's William's go on the ladder when I've had enough."

So, not grumbling out loud this time, they turned their attention to the overgrown mass of grass, weeds and bushes.

"You said we could scythe the grass," said William. His face had lit up slightly.

"We haven't got a scythe yet," Mum replied. "And don't think we're going to let *you* loose on your own with it when we do. No, just have a look and see how bad it really is. We'll probably end by digging the whole lot up with a rotavator, but have a look anyway."

William shrugged his shoulders. "That means you don't trust us to do anything," he muttered.

They pushed their way into the garden. Rosy saw the long grass, the weeds striving for the sun within it, heard the hum of insects, saw bees round tiny flowers she had never seen before, and called back to Mum, "Nobody's touched this for years. The fields round about have been ploughed and grazed all that time. There must be rare plants here. We shouldn't dig it up."

Dad heard her. "We've bought a garden, not a nature reserve. It's all got to come up." Then, relenting, "I see what you mean. We'll keep a corner for Nature."

Content with that, Rosy picked her way through knee- and waist-high weeds. Then she stopped.

"There was a path here once," she said.

Beneath her feet were the remains of a brick path, now crumbled beyond repair. She had a vision of the strip of concrete which, no doubt, would one day take its place. She followed the path up the garden. William rushed past her to lead the way. Louise tagged behind Rosy.

The path disappeared into the bushes.

"So once the path went right through the shrubbery," said Rosy.

"But does it lead to anything?" said William.

He started to push through the bushes.

"Don't go, William," cried Louise. "You don't know what's in there. It might be dangerous."

William took Louise's warning as a challenge. For almost the first time since they had been in Dyson's Cottage, he looked enthusiastic.

"I'm going through," he announced. "It'd be better with a knife to hack a path but I'll manage."

He started to push at the branches: they sprang back at him and scratched his face.

"They don't want me in here," he said. "The bushes are like the house. Well, I don't care. I'm going in."

He shoved, grunted and swore his way out of their sight. The branches were so thick that soon they could not see him at all. But his voice and the crashing, tearing and splitting of branches and clothes stayed very close.

Within a few minutes, he called from inside the mass.

"It's no use. I can't get any further. I'm coming out."

He scrambled back. His face and hands were torn and bleeding, his sweatshirt was ripped and little leaves and twigs stuck to him. Louise laughed.

"Mum'll go crazy when she sees you," said Rosy.

"Why? We came here to work, didn't we? That means getting dirty."

"What did you see, William?" said Louise.

"Nothing. The bushes wouldn't let me."

"Oh, don't start that rubbish again," said Rosy.

"But I mean it. They wouldn't. They get thicker. It's like a barrier surrounding something we're not allowed to see."

"Like Sleeping Beauty's castle?" Louise asked.

"There are no secrets in a mass of old bushes," said Rosy.

"Oh, yes, there are," William replied. "Why wouldn't they let me go any further? They don't want us here, just like the house."

Suddenly, Rosy had had enough of this. She turned on William angrily. "Just shut up!" she shouted. "You may think that's all funny, but it's just making trouble."

William stared at her. "But I'm not making trouble, Rosy," he said. "It's true."

Chapter 7

They finally called it a day at half-past six. Mum had announced earlier that they would take turns with the cooking: Dad and William would not escape. But for now, she and Rosy would start off their first proper meal. Cooking spaghetti and making a proper meat sauce over the little gas rings on the camping stove took a long time. "The sooner this place is all rewired, the better," said Dad.

Nevertheless, he was obviously feeling pleased with himself. The roof was weathertight, the tiles all fixed and the felt underneath fit to last a few more years yet. He had been up to the loft and found the joists underneath free of rot. He had come down again with the same refrain: "The last people here worked very hard before they left. Why ever did they go?"

After supper, as dusk fell, there was more discontent. Louise complained again about the lack of a television.

"I want one," she said. "It would stop me thinking about all the things."

"What things, Louise?" Mum said.

"The things in the house. The ones that are whispering at us."

"Oh, don't be silly." said Mum. "Play your tapes."

"Heard them all. I'm sick of them."

Her voice was so dull, so dispirited, so unlike the usual bubbly Louise. Mum took a quick glance at Dad, who glanced back, opened his mouth as if to speak, then shut it again. Rosy had a good idea of what he might have said. So she said it for him, even if she didn't quite believe it.

"Louise, there's nothing here that's whispering. It's your imagination telling you things in an old house. You must stop thinking about yourself all the time. We're all having a bad time. We've got to pull together until it's better."

"Thank you, Rosy," Mum murmured.

"I still want my television," Louise grumbled.

Rosy remembered something.

"Didn't we pack some games? Let's play them."

"After we've cleared away," said Mum. "And Louise can help wash up."

When everything was put away and the table washed down, Rosy looked for the games. "It's Monopoly, Cluedo or cards," she announced.

There was immediate argument. "I wanted television so I should have first pick," said Louise.

"You can," said Mum. "But it's because you're the youngest, not because you were cross."

"Cluedo," said Louise.

Dad lit a Tilley lamp and the shadows round them deepened into darkness. Soon, all of them had done Dr Black to death with different weapons several times in various rooms of the house and they seemed much happier. Until Louise said, "I'm still frightened. There's people with guns and rope and bits of piping hiding in the dark waiting to get us. And they're whispering again."

"Please don't be so silly, Louise," said Mum patiently.

But is she silly? wondered Rosy. *Is this not what I felt last night and what William feels when he says the house doesn't like us? And who's to say Mum and Dad don't feel it too but won't say. And why did the people here before leave when they'd nearly made the house all right again? But why do I feel I'm home, I'm meant to be here? It's all so difficult. I wish we weren't in this awful place.*

It was no use continuing with the game. Louise's outburst had taken all the pleasure away. Darkness had fallen now outside – and beyond the little yellow light cast by the Tilley lamp, it was dark inside as well. Rosy shivered. She could not remember being anywhere, except in a tent, where she could not dispel darkness completely by a flick of a switch. Louise could almost be right. What lurked behind the door, in the passageway, not three metres away but smothered in inky blackness?

She shook herself. Nothing, that's what. Don't be stupid.

"Monopoly, I think," said Dad. "At least nobody's going to get savagely murdered in that, only bankrupted."

They packed the Cluedo away. Rosy put it back and brought out the Monopoly. As they set it up she saw, like last night, tiny moths fluttering round the lamp. For a moment there was no talking: the creaks and cries of the house and outside were very clear.

"I see what you mean about whispering, Louise," said Mum.

"But they aren't whispering now," said Louise. "That's not what I meant."

"Come on, let's start," said Dad, too heartily.

Beyond the lamp, behind Mum's shoulders, over Louise's head as she arranged her money, beyond William and Dad either side of her, Rosy seemed to see the moving shadows.

The house is alive. We try to knock it into submission during the day, but at night it shows it has a mind of its own and won't go to sleep.

It was an ugly thought. Doubly so when Rosy realized that however alive the house was, they were fated to try sleeping in it for years to come.

Monopoly had petered out after barely half an hour. Plainly Rosy wasn't alone in what she felt, though nobody gave voice to it.

Except, after Louise had said she'd had enough games for that night and Mum said it was getting late and they ought to get to bed because there would be more hard work tomorrow, William had stood up and spoken, slowly and deliberately.

"I told you. This house doesn't like us."

"Oh, shut up, William," said Mum. "Louise is bad enough. Please don't talk rubbish."

"It's not rubbish. It's true. Why won't anyone listen to me?"

Nobody said any more. Except that Louise, as she, Rosy and William prepared their sleeping bags in the front room, began to cry.

Rosy quickly put an arm around her shoulders. "It will be all right, Louise. Really it will."

"I don't like it here," Louise snuffled. "I'm frightened. I want to go home."

"So do I. But we can't." Already, Rosy thought, the new people would be in, the house full of different furniture, plans would be being made to change all their familiar wallpaper. Some girl she would never meet would just be going to sleep in her old room decorated the way she'd wanted it, saying, "As soon as I can I'm changing this lot."

Yes, they really were *trapped*. Of course, Rosy had known this was no holiday, this was for real and for ever – but until that very moment she hadn't really *felt* it, *known* its truth course all round her body, flood her brain. *This is it, this is how it will be for ever.*

She burrowed down in her sleeping bag, wanting to cover herself right up as protection from this moving, shadowy, rustling place. Louise was right. It whispered.

But she couldn't. It was her job to look after the lamp.

"Are you reading tonight, William?" she asked.

There was silence. Then: "No. I'm too fed up."

"Then I'll put the lamp out."

She waited. There was no cry from Louise of "Not yet!" So within a second, a pitch darkness hit them like a soft but smothering animal. Outside, owls occasionally screeched, vixens gave their high yap, cattle in the field lowed. The house noises, like whisperings magnified, sounded as if deep inside her ears before she covered herself with the sleeping bag. *I'll never sleep*, she thought. But she did. Her last thought was, *No wonder Louise is frightened of the whispering,* before she was in a deep slumber. And it was as if she opened her eyes at once, to a dream of staggering clarity.

Chapter 8

She stood in sunshine, with warmth on her back. To one side of her was a vegetable garden. She saw potatoes in rows growing leafy and green out of their straight earth ridges. Cabbages stood in lines like tiny soldiers. Beyond were peas, then runner beans streaked with flowering red climbed profusely up their high stick framework. There was not a weed to be seen. Along this little place of plenty was a path, made of blue bricks set neatly into the ground. On the other side was a chicken house with a large, covered run. She heard clucking and saw the birds run round inside, pecking their seed and preening themselves. The whole showed that someone had worked very hard to make this a neat and productive place.

She looked behind her. Yes. It was the house, windows smart and shining, paint uncracked and unblistered, bricks freshly pointed. A wisp of smoke climbed from the chimney pot. A tin bath hung from the back wall. The paved yard was empty except for the logs stacked against the outhouse wall.

She was outside their own house. But how had it reached this state of perfection? Was she seeing it as one day it would be? If so, why was that tin bath there?

She was not alone. Someone stood next to her. She looked round to see who it was. But the person must have at once stepped behind her. Each time she turned, there was no one there. Yet, always, she was sure someone stood beside her – someone she could never quite see.

"Where are you?" she tried to say. But she could utter no words: her voice seemed unable to work. She tried to walk forward, but she was rooted to the spot. She felt sudden panic.

Then a soft hand took hers, squeezed it. She felt flooded with warmth, peace. She squeezed it back.

The hand guided her. She turned and looked at the garden again. Someone was in it: she saw a figure bending, back to her, picking peas, putting them in a basket. As she watched, the figure straightened. A woman, in a white apron, hair pinned back. Not young. Face worn with hard work and worry. She looked at Rosy – but no, she was not looking at Rosy. She was looking at whoever was beside her. She made an angry gesture as if to make her move on. Then she looked beyond the two of them – if two there were. Her face was contorted with fear – and warning.

Now Rosy felt the hands guiding her, pulling her along. She could move at last. She and her unseen companion glided away – swiftly down the path towards the bushes.

A voice beside her spoke – in a whisper, so she could not tell what manner of person it was. "I must get on. I must not just stand here. It is wrong."

And then Rosy knew something else – another voice behind her. A loud voice, a man's voice, an angry, savage voice. It roared, slurred and indistinct, but she knew it cursed her, threatened her and that to hear it day after day would shrivel her soul and make her die.

Fear, despondency and complete, utter hopelessness overwhelmed her. She gripped the hand of her unseen companion harder than ever. But she knew neither of them could give comfort to the other because matters were far too terrible for hope or escape.

She woke. It was morning: sunlight filtered through the makeshift curtains. William and Louise still slept.

She looked back over her dream. Yes, it had indeed been very clear. But what was it a dream of? Who were these people? Did those she saw, heard and felt *really exist*? In the past? The future? For that was certainly this house she had stood outside. But very different from how it was now.

And what about the terrible feeling she had

had at the end? With a shock, she realized it hadn't gone away. She *still* felt despondent and hopeless. But was that because over the last days she had been despondent and hopeless anyway? And there was fear there as well. Had she felt fear before? She didn't know: couldn't be sure. So what she still felt – were these real feelings or dream feelings? Were they hers – *or somebody else's?*

And yet from the very start, from the moment she'd seen this house, there had been that feeling underneath – *this is yours, you were meant to come here.* Ah, but was that a comfort? Or was it a warning and threat as much as those of the man with the angry voice?

She didn't know. But that dream was *very* real.

William woke. He sat up, looked at her. Then he spoke – words which made her head spin.

"Rosy," he said. "Where did you go last night?"

"What do you mean?"

"I saw you. You got up in the middle of the

night. You went outside. I just thought you were going to the loo, but you didn't come back. So I got out and took my torch in case something had happened. And I saw you standing on the path. Who was that you were with?"

"Don't be silly, William. You were dreaming. I never got up last night."

William's mouth shut in a straight line. He looked very angry.

He waited a few seconds before he spoke again.

"Don't try and tell me whether I'm dreaming or not. You got up, went out of this house, stood on the path and someone stood next to you. I saw it, as sure as I'm in this room now. I won't have you making out I'm some sort of nutcase because I'm not. I know what I saw. And if you don't own up to it, it's because you don't want anybody to know. Do you want me to tell Mum and Dad?"

"Tell who you like, William. I slept all night. They'll just say you're making trouble."

William threw himself down on his sleeping bag.

"I hate this rotten place," he muttered. "And I hate you with it. The whole lot of you."

Rosy lay back on her elbows. It was no use just cutting William off like that. After all, what he said he had seen was, in a sort of way, right. But she *had* been dreaming. Hadn't she? Yes, of course she had. Where she had been was nothing like what was there now. And it was broad daylight in the dream: the sun was shining. The figure William had seen was in the dark.

But what he had said was right. How could he have known unless he had been there? Or had the same dream himself?

Something was happening which was just too much for her to understand. How was it going to end?

She got out of her sleeping bag and trailed miserably off through the kitchen into the bathroom.

Chapter 9

After breakfast, before Mum gave out the day's jobs, Rosy slipped outside on her own. She stood where she had been standing in her dream and looked round. She recognized it all. There, where tangled greenery now sighed in the morning breeze, had been that trim, weedless vegetable patch: dark earth and straight rows of plants. On the other side of the path she could so easily imagine the chicken run: suddenly, she fancied she could hear scratchings and clucks from contented birds. The ruined path, so unlike the deep-set, iron-grey bricks of the dream, stretched away from her to the jungle at the end. She walked down it, to where the briars and branches stood thickly, repelling her, daring her to push through further. She had that feeling again – that beyond the impenetrable screen lay a Holy Grail, a treasure concealed from prying eyes.

Daft. Treasure? Here? She turned round and looked back at the house.

She caught her breath in shock. It couldn't be. Yes, it was. In the middle of the weeds stood a young, smocked figure: a girl with long, dark, tousled hair. She was bending as if picking some crop no longer there. Then she straightened up and looked at Rosy.

And smiled as if in recognition.

Rosy, baffled, started to run towards her.

Then she blinked. The figure was gone.

My imagination, she thought. *The dream was so real I'm still in it.*

But those homely noises from the chicken run still worried at her ears: she *could* hear them, she *could*.

No, she thought. *There must be big birds, partridges or pheasants, nesting just over the fence in the field. They probably sound like chickens. I just can't see them from here.*

And then, from the house, came that same man's voice, angry, slurred, cursing. *What's happening in there?* was her first thought. *Has Dad lost his temper? The house must really be getting to him.* She dashed along the path and indoors. But what did she find there but Dad measuring the skirting boards, Mum showing Louise how to fold up the camping table they had been eating at, and William staring moodily out of the window.

The voice left her, with a hollow echo like the door of a tomb being slammed shut. All was silent.

She stood unable to speak, to think. She was cold: the hair at the back of her neck prickled. She thought she would faint. She swayed, sat down on a stool and put her head in her hands.

William stopped looking out of the window. He turned on his heel and stalked into the hallway. Rosy suddenly wanted to talk to him, to sort out what he thought had happened last night, to get him out of the depression he was in, to make him feel all right again...

She followed him into the hallway. He was standing at the foot of the stairs which Dad wouldn't let them go up. He looked at her without hostility. Rosy felt thankful. He spoke.

"I don't care what Dad says. I'm going up to see what's there."

"I'll come with you," said Rosy. Mum and Dad were fed up enough with William already: it wasn't fair that if any trouble was going to be got into, he should cop it all on his own.

So they crept cautiously up the stairs. William felt each wooden step with his feet before stepping on it. "This one's dodgy," he would say, or "Miss that one out." At the top, they looked down.

"It's not that bad," said William. "What's all the fuss about?"

"I was wondering whether, if the house hates us so much, it might make sure its stairs collapse beneath us," said Rosy. She couldn't quite keep the sarcasm out of her voice.

"Shut up," said William. "It's not the house I worry about now."

They were standing on the bare boards of the landing. Each side of them was a door: another, narrower door faced them at the end. William opened the door of the room which looked out of the front of the house.

Light flooded in through the two windows. The room was long, taking up the whole width of the house. The dirty floorboards were bare, cobwebs festooned the ceiling and peeling walls. A choked fireplace was at one end where the wall bellied out to show where the chimney was.

"This must be the one Dad's going to build the wall across," said Rosy.

"The two rooms will still be pretty big," William replied. "They'll probably give one of them to you."

"I might like one of the back rooms better," said Rosy.

William said nothing. Then he looked at her keenly and said, "Come on. You can tell me up here. You *did* go outside last night, didn't you?"

"*No*, William," she replied. She considered for a moment, then, as his face tightened up angrily again, "But I did have a dream. A very real one. I *dreamt* I was outside the house."

"You didn't dream it. You were *there.*"

His face was so earnest that she had to believe he meant what he said. But she daren't even think about why he meant it.

"Oh, William," she said. "What does it all mean?"

He didn't answer. He walked out of the room back to the landing and opened the door opposite.

Another separate room with one window looking over the garden. William peered through the filthy glass. He wiped a clear patch with his hands and looked with interest at the black dirt which now covered them. Then he turned and surveyed the floor, walls, fireplace, brown ceiling with the single frayed light flex dangling from it.

"Not bad as this place goes," he said. "It has possibilities."

"You're beginning to talk like Dad," said Rosy.

"When you're stuck on the bottom, the

only way is up."

Back out on the landing, they looked at the final, smaller door. William opened it.

"Let's see what Louise will have to put up with," he said.

He opened it. The door creaked as if not properly set on its hinges. A musty smell emerged, far stronger than from the other rooms. The room was very small and, oddly, cold.

"Look, no fireplace," said William.

"Are you sure it *is* a bedroom?" said Rosy. "It's not just a big cupboard, is it?"

And then her stomach turned. Because she felt a hand take hers, reach for her fingers, then curl around her palms and gently squeeze them. Just as in the dream. And she found herself saying, "Yes, William. It *is* a bedroom. I know it now."

She did not say, but now she knew something else as well. Someone had been very unhappy in it.

As they crept cautiously back downstairs, William said, "Don't you think it's strange?

Whoever was here before did work downstairs and up on the roof. But they didn't seem to touch upstairs at all. You'd think mending the stairs would have been the first thing they did."

Something drove them out of this house, Rosy thought but did not say. *Something which stopped them going up the stairs. And at this rate we'll be driven out as well.*

At the foot of the stairs stood Louise, watching them. Mum and Dad were outside inspecting pipes and clearing gutters. Louise's face was angry.

"It's not fair. Why didn't you take me upstairs with you?"

"Because it's not safe," said Rosy.

"Yes, it is. You're bigger than me and you didn't fall through."

"It's too scary," said William. "You'd have been so frightened you'd have cried."

She'll say "I don't believe you" now and try to push past, Rosy thought. But she didn't. She looked at William with absolute belief in her eyes. It just showed, Rosy thought, what the last two days must have been like for her.

"Don't listen to him, Louise," she said. "It's just dirty up there."

She would tell nobody what she had felt in the little room.

"Don't tell Mum and Dad we were upstairs, Louise," said William. "Or you'll be sorry."

Chapter 10

Louise said nothing. Half of her believed what William had said. She couldn't forget the sudden chill that had seized her the day they came and that she had gripped Mummy's hand and said, "I'm frightened." Because she had been. She had looked at the lonely, unhappy house which didn't want them there. She had known that to go in there – *and* stay – would upset it, make it do nasty things to get rid of them.

Yet it hadn't been quite so bad since. After all, they were all together – and while everyone was there, no harm could come. But each night before she slept, she curled herself up in a little ball like a scared hedgehog, to keep the dark away and shut out the whispering voices which rushed and rustled through the air and tried to say things to her that she didn't want to hear. Yet both nights so far she had managed to sleep, quickly and well. What a mercy. What frightened her most was that one night soon, she wouldn't.

The day wore to its close. Louise couldn't help with the gutters because they wouldn't let her go up the ladders. After a moment's sulking she decided she was pleased about that and even more pleased that she didn't have to touch the dirty and squelchy old leaves Mum and Dad – and later, William and Rosy – scooped out of them. Most of the day she spent with either Mum or Rosy washing walls down and scrubbing floors. Everything looked and smelt nicer when they had finished. Louise looked round with pride: even though she was only seven, they couldn't have done this without her.

Supper, games, listening to the little radio, sighing for television – then came the moment each night that Louise now dreaded. She, William and Rosy were in that dark front room with just the Tilley lamp for light and airbed and sleeping bag for comfort. And once again she snuggled deep down for protection.

And this time she knew inside that once Rosy had put the Tilley lamp off, sleep would not come so quickly.

Tonight, the whisperers seemed determined to make her hear them. She covered her ears – and it was as if other, invisible, icy fingers were pulling hers away. Weightless, bodiless people she could not see were fighting over her.

She wanted to cry out. But William and Rosy were asleep already. The very thought of getting up and tiptoeing out to Mum and Dad made her stomach turn to jelly. She would never get there. The invisible spirits would curl their long, strong arms round her and that would be the end of her. She *knew*.

For hours she lay, whimpering slightly in fear. And then, somehow or other, she managed to doze.

She woke. Outside, the moon was up: grey

light filtered through the windows and showed the sleeping forms of William and Rosy. The voices had gone: the room was still and quiet.

But not, she suddenly realized, empty. She blinked, but what she saw did not go away. A form, grey and indistinct in the unreal moonlight, bent over Rosy's sleeping bag.

"Mummy?" Louise whispered. "Is Rosy all right?"

The figure made no sign of hearing.

Louise tried again. "Rosy?" she said, slightly louder.

The grey figure straightened up and looked directly at her.

Louise caught her breath.

It was not Mummy. IT WAS ROSY.

But how could this be? Rosy was asleep in her sleeping bag. She *knew* that: even as she watched, Rosy stirred and muttered in her sleep.

BUT IT WAS CERTAIN THAT THE GIRL STANDING OVER ROSY *WAS* ROSY.

But another Rosy. The new Rosy had the

same brown eyes but her hair was tousled and longer. Her face was thinner.

Just as Louise was wondering how it was that she could tell the new Rosy's eyes were brown in the grey, moonlit half-darkness, the Rosy she knew stirred again, sat up, clasped her double's hand as if she had been waiting for her and it was the most natural thing in the world. Then she rose out of the sleeping bag. For a moment the two stood together – one with shoulder-length neat hair, the other with hair straggling uncared-for down her back: one in a new nightdress, the other in a shapeless smock. But otherwise – identical, doubles: to Louise, exactly the same person seen twice.

She sat up in her sleeping bag, not daring to breathe. The two Rosies moved out of the room, the Rosy wearing the smock leading the Rosy Louise knew by the hand. They hesitated in front of the door: then Louise's Rosy reached forward and opened it. A strange thought crossed Louise's mind: *would the new Rosy have needed it open?*

They were gone. Louise was on the point of

sinking back, trembling, into her sleeping bag. Then – *no: I have to follow.* Gulping down her fear, she unzipped the side of her sleeping bag and stood up. The night air struck cold even inside the room. She snatched up her anorak and pulled it on. She reached for her torch – then thought better of it. *They must not know she was there.*

Louise slipped into the hallway. She heard the back door open. She darted into the scullery. The one cold tap dripped sullenly into the stone sink. The back door remained ajar. Louise cautiously looked through it into the garden.

The night breeze breathed fresh on her face. Marston Woods stood dark and mysterious to one side: the wide fields on the other. Three cows had come to the fence: Louise heard their jaws champing as they grazed and could see their breath like little clouds as they incuriously watched.

But what took all Louise's attention was in front of her in the garden. Rosy was there, a dark shadow stealthy in the long grass. But the visitor stood next to her clear as day for all the darkness: it was more than moonlight which let Louise see the old, torn smock and the long, uncombed hair.

Louise gulped, felt her heart hammer. She nearly turned and ran back indoors.

But no. She would force herself to wait and watch. At the very back of her mind was a strange feeling that what she saw now was what they had come to Dyson's Cottage for.

Chapter 11

William slept soundly. But as the night wore on, dreams overtook him. They were not good dreams. They were dark dreams in which harsh voices spoke to him of things he had never thought of. But when he heard these words and considered them in his slumber, his mind said, "That's right. Why have I never realized that before?" He heard shrieks, screams, shouts; he saw beseeching faces, bruised and cowering bodies; he felt as he slept anger which would not die when he woke. He shook and moaned in his sleeping bag. The harsh voices said to him, "See, William? It is for you now as it was for us then. You know what to do, don't you?" And

William in his dream said, "Yes, I do. And when I wake I will not forget."

Who would soothe him out of his new and ugly feelings. His parents? But Mum and Dad were even now dreaming dreams which were similar, which would make them see the world in a way much different from what they had gone to bed with.

The two Rosies drifted away from Louise. They moved down the brick path between the weeds. Louise plucked up courage and followed them. The cows across the fence raised their eyes and watched them, then turned again to their grazing.

The two Rosies had reached the overgrown bushes. They stopped. Louise stopped too, about ten metres away. She was sure they had no idea she was there. They looked at the bushes as if making a decision. Then they disappeared into them. Louise saw the new girl appear to drift through them: she heard the rustle of leaves and the breaking of twigs as Rosy pushed them aside and forced her way through.

She'll be all scratches and her nightie will be torn in the morning, Louise thought.

She stood and watched. The two were now hidden completely. She thought: *What's the point of this? I have to go in there as well.*

She shivered. She remembered what Rosy had said on their first afternoon there. The bushes were a barrier to something "like Sleeping Beauty's castle". *No, I can't go in. I'll wait here for them to come out again.*

Then she heard another noise. From within the bushes was the sound of crying – deep, racking sobs.

Was it Rosy? Now she *had* to go in. Plucking up every bit of courage she possessed, she started to push through the bushes, not caring if thorns scratched her face and tore at her legs.

Soon, she had to fight hard to pierce the barrier to what the bushes hid from view. But always the crying led her on. Rosy had got through, so she could. William hadn't made it on that first day here, but he'd broken enough branches to make it possible for both of them. And at last she made it. She burst through the springy branches and briars and found herself in a clearing.

For a moment, she could not make out what had happened. Things were different here. It was brighter: everything seemed clear as day. But the light was not that of the sun. *Could the moon shine like this?* For here, every detail could be picked out in perfect dream-like clarity.

The crying had stopped. But Louise could not at once see Rosy and her companion. What filled Louise's vision was the un-expected structure in the middle of the clearing. A low, circular brick wall forming the surround of a deep shaft. From the wall rose wooden columns supporting a tiled roof. Over the shaft was a handle. Its spindle was coiled with rope, one end of which dropped straight down the shaft. Greatly daring, Louise crept to the edge of the wall and looked down. Below her, the shaft stretched seemingly to infinity. Cold and a brackish smell rose to meet her.

A well, she thought. *Nobody ever said there was a well here.*

Now she crouched behind the wall, willing herself not to run for the safety of the bushes. There was silence. Even the noises of the night from the woods and fields had died away. She lifted her head – and saw the two Rosies.

They still held hands. They stood on the other side of the well looking over the surround. They peered into its depths.

And now the crying started again. The sobs seemed to reach deep into Louise's ears and she clapped her hands over them to keep such grief out. But it was the newcomer who cried, not Rosy. Rosy put her arm around her companion's shoulders and gradually the crying died away. Louise could take her hands from her ears.

Together, the two continued to look down into the blackness where, Louise presumed, was water and a pail at the end of the rope to draw it up in. And, it seemed, there must be something else. The identical faces of the two frowned, their brows knitted, as if what lay below, which they sought so earnestly, mattered more than anything in the world.

Louise, breathless, waited.

The two straightened up. They looked at each other. They seemed both to nod their heads, as if in agreement about something. Then they walked together round the well, passing not one metre away from Louise but showing no sign that they knew she was there. They passed through the bushes again, the new Rosy silently, Louise's Rosy with the same cracking and rustling of branches.

Louise was about to follow. But she stopped. *What had Rosy been shown that lay at the bottom of the well?*

Fearfully, Louise rose. She gripped her fingers round the cold, hard bricks. She saw where, on the inside, these bricks were stained green, and where, hardly a metre below her, they disappeared in formless dark. The rope from the handle dropped invisible in the same darkness. The brackish smell rose stronger than ever to her nose.

She found a little stone by her feet. She dropped it over the side. She waited. A second later, a tiny splash echoed and the sound, magnifying itself as it rebounded off the brick sides on its way up, returned to her.

She leant over again and looked down. Daringly she spoke.

"Hello?"

Her voice echoed back and seemed to repeat itself round her ears until she thought she was surrounded by dozens of invisible Louises all trying to greet her.

Then both splash and voice died away and in the silence she strained her eyes to make out any detail deep in the shaft.

There was nothing she could see but the blackness into which everything disappeared.

She stepped back, trembling slightly. Then she turned, blundering through the bushes and, once through them, stopped for breath on the brick path.

She was back in the cold, grey half-light of the moon. There was no sign of Rosy or her companion.

Suddenly, all Louise wanted was to be back in her sleeping bag. She ran hard up the path, only now aware of the stings and scratches the bushes had given her. Once at the house, she stopped. The scullery door was still open: she closed it gently behind her. She tiptoed into their room – just in time to see Rosy lift up the side of her sleeping bag and slide quietly into it.

"Rosy, are you all right?" she whispered.

Rosy made no answer. She lay down and was at once asleep.

Louise crept back into her sleeping bag. She pulled up the zip at the side and the little plastic rasp sounded loud like the tearing of sheets. She lay, still smarting with the touch of the thorns and briars, and tried to think back on all that had happened to her.

But not for long. Soon she too was asleep – and, like the others, she had strange, disturbing, unwelcome dreams. Cruel, twisted faces leered at her, harsh voices spoke to her. "What you've seen means misery for you all. Don't trust your half-sister and the visions she shows you."

Only the morning sunshine broke into her sleep. When she woke, Louise was troubled. She knew something terrible had happened but she did not know what it meant. Except that things would not be the same again.

* * *

For Mum, Dad and William, sleep had gone on. When the same sunshine woke them, they too would see the world very differently.

Chapter 12

The family sat round the table eating breakfast. Nobody spoke. William glowered at his toast, picking at his cornflakes. Dad stared fixedly at the window, as if he had already knocked the frames out but had forgotten to buy anything to replace them. Mum, strangely for her, ate voraciously, as if she had been starving.

Louise had to break the silence.

"There's a well behind the bushes," she announced.

Mum stopped chewing. "I never knew that," she said.

"Oh yes," said Louise.

Dad tore his eyes away from the window

and looked angrily at her. "Don't be silly, Louise," he said. "I don't like it when you kids deliberately stir up trouble by telling lies."

"But there *is*." Louise felt tears sting the backs of her eyes. "I *saw* it. Rosy and I were there last night."

Rosy looked blank. "What are you talking about?" she said.

William looked up from his plate. "I told you, but you wouldn't believe me," he said. "Rosy gets up each night and wanders off with her new friends." Dad stood up. Louise watched him. She remembered her dream and could not be surprised at what happened next. Sheer fury creased his face. He stood over Rosy and shouted, "Everything that's wrong in this place comes down to *you*. Rosy this, Rosy that, Rosy sleepwalking every night, Rosy with all the problems. Well, things have got to change. I won't have this any more. And I won't have your so-called friends trespassing here at night."

He sat down again abruptly.

Rosy cowered back, shocked. What had

happened? This wasn't like the Dad she'd loved and trusted all her remembered life. She looked from one to the other. William looked back and broke into a sneering laugh. Mum was regarding her with distaste, as she would a dead rat. And what about dear Louise?

Louise spoke again. She felt suddenly happy. Nobody was cross with her any more.

"Let's all go outside," she said. "I'll show you the well."

After breakfast, Louise led the way up the brick path. The rest followed in a straight line, Rosy at the back, fearful of what might happen. They stood where the bushes took over the end of the garden.

"Look," said Louise. "Here's where we pushed through. You can see where the branches are all broken."

Indeed, the white of broken wood was a clear sign of Louise's struggle in the night.

"I'll do better than that," said Dad.

He ran back to the house and brought back a saw and secateurs. He and Mum started to clear a way through. Right through to the dense middle of the thicket and beyond they sliced their way.

"There," said Dad. "Satisfied?"

There was no well. There was not even a clearing. All that existed at the end of the garden was a mass of wild, overgrown, tangled bushes which choked everything they covered.

"You dreamt it, love," said Mum, looking at Louise fondly.

"I *didn't*. Did I, Rosy?" Louise was nearly crying with frustration. The voice in the dream, which she could still hear echoing inside her head, was right. Rosy's visions meant misery for them all. And it was starting here. Rosy, tight-lipped, said nothing. "Tell them, Rosy" Louise insisted. "We were here."

"Don't ask *her* anything," said William.

Louise's face creased with temper. "You *tricked* me, Rosy," she shouted. "I *hate* you."

Grey clouds were massing. The sun went in. Everybody shivered in the air's new chill. The morning's bright promise was gone. But it was not only the weather which had changed. Rosy felt chilled inside. People who had loved her seemed overnight to hate her. It was too much to take or understand. Rosy knew the coldness round about her was as much in the people she lived with, and it meant the whole basis of her life was suddenly, mystifyingly, ruined.

William went on. "You tell us, Louise. We'll believe *you*."

So Louise told them about everything that had happened to her, ending with, "And the girl she was with, she was just like her. She was another Rosy. She *was*. Where does she live, Rosy. Is she near here?"

Everybody looked at Rosy.

"Well?" said Dad roughly. "Is she? Have you got some friend you've not told us about? Some long-lost relation who breaks in every night?"

"I don't know what Louise is talking about," Rosy managed to mutter. Louise stepped back, as if Rosy had slapped her across the face.

"Louder, girl," said Dad. "We can't hear you."

"I don't..." Rosy began.

William interrupted. "That's twice in two nights. She's got secrets she won't tell us about."

Rosy looked from one to the other. Her heart sank with foreknowledge of what her life ahead would be like.

The trouble was, she *did* know what Louise was talking about. The memory of looking down the slimy, wet brick sides of a deep well shaft for something just beyond the reach of sight was very clear to her. But it was a *dream*, just like the night before. She had walked with a companion she never saw, whose name she didn't know. She had felt her companion's misery. She had known that whatever it was she could not see in the well *mattered* and was the most important thing in the world. She knew also that her companion would have told her what it was if she had been able to. But though she had known her feelings, she had not known her meanings. They would come later. For now, she knew only that she was the only one who could help her new companion. But how?

When she woke up, those feelings were still with her. But it didn't matter what William and Louise said. THESE WERE ONLY DREAMS. Weren't they?

"I don't know what's happening," said Rosy. "Please help me."

She looked in turn at the four people round her – Mum, Dad, William and Louise. All four looked stonily back.

"I'm tired of this," said Dad. "There's a mountain of work to be done and I'm going back to the house." He turned on his heel and marched back along the path, Mum following.

Once they were gone, the other two set about Rosy.

"Why did you say that?" cried Louise. "There *was* a well. We were all there. You, me and that girl."

"All you're doing is getting Louise and me into trouble," William shouted. "I saw this girl too, remember. You're just a liar."

Rosy wouldn't listen to any more. She stumbled away through the weeds towards the fence and leaned breathless on it, looking out far away across the field.

What was happening to her? Why had everybody turned against her? Tears blinded her eyes and the field in front of her became blurred.

Then she was aware of something beside her. Someone else was leaning on the fence – and she knew it was a friend, someone who could help her. William? Louise? Could they have thought better of what they'd said and come to make it up? She turned gratefully.

There was no one there. She closed her eyes in despair.

But then she seemed to hear a voice, deep in her ear – the small, quiet, gentle voice of a girl. "Rosy, these were not dreams. We did walk in the garden, you and I, these last two nights."

Rosy shook her head angrily. "Go away," she said aloud. "I don't know who you are."

"I know. I'm beyond your reach. You won't know who I am – not yet. You must find me. When you have found me, you must save me. But you cannot save me until you have suffered what I suffered."

Rosy's despair grew, like a dark formless mass standing the other side of her.

"I'm suffering already," she said.

"This is nothing yet. There are more ghosts here than me, Rosy. They are strong ghosts. Perhaps they are stronger than me. They will fight you hard. They have strong weapons. They will not let me find you if they can help it."

"I don't know what you mean," said Rosy.

"You will, you will."

Suddenly, Rosy was angry with herself. What was she doing, leaning over the fence talking to somebody who wasn't there? She shook her head angrily, to clear the madness away. "SHUT UP!" she shouted.

There was silence. Her companion was gone. Now she was sorry she had shouted. She wanted to call, "Come back. Tell me more."

But it was too late. William and Louise stood by her.

"Talking to yourself?" said William mockingly.

"Please. You must help me," said Rosy. "I think I'm being haunted."

"Rubbish," said William.

"You made us look silly," said Louise.

"I wish you didn't live with us," said William.

With a sudden sob, Rosy turned away from them and ran towards the refuge of the house.

Refuge? Since they had arrived here, she had never lost that feeling that this place had been waiting for her, that it was where she ought to be. No longer, though. Everything was changed. The windows like blank eyes, the door like a closed mouth, stared back at her threateningly. "Keep out, Rosy," they seemed to say.

Chapter 13

A voice sounded. Dad's.

"I've got to go to town. I need to buy all the electrical stuff for the wiring. And a lot else besides. Are you coming, William and Louise? Help me hitch up the trailer."

The two rushed eagerly to where the green Vauxhall stood.

Rosy watched them lifting the trailer so Dad could couple it to the car. They looked somehow complete together. Suddenly she was the outsider. It was a terrible feeling.

"What about me?" she managed to say.

"Don't let her come. She ruins everything," shouted Louise.

Dad looked at Rosy as if she was a stranger.

She flinched under the stony blankness of his gaze. He did not speak for a moment: the silence seemed to tie itself round her head like a tight knot.

At last he spoke. "Get in. We'll need someone to shift the heavy stuff."

Louise rushed for the front seat of the car. William, grumbling, belted himself in at the back and spent the whole journey exaggeratedly separating himself from Rosy as if she gave out bad smells.

Rosy sat miserably as they bumped their way over the track. Louise got out to open the gate as if this was now her regular routine: then they passed along the road with its high hedges. Under the steely grey clouds there was very little that seemed pleasant about Great Marston today as they descended the hill towards the town centre. The industrial estate where the builders' merchants was looked bleak, windswept and half-derelict.

The errand here meant visits to many departments. Dad wanted bags of ready-mixed concrete and mortar and several lengths of prepared wood as well as all the cable, sockets and circuit-breakers for wiring the cottage. When the concrete in its re-inforced paper bags had been loaded into the trailer and Dad had been given the dockets for payment, and after all the wood and the electrical goods had been selected, they went to the payment counter. William and Louise walked happily together. Rosy heaved alone at the trolley with its awkward load of long wood boards. Dad strode behind like an overseer.

The man behind the counter seemed kind, Rosy thought.

"You're the people from Dyson's Cottage, aren't you?" he said.

"Yes," Dad replied. "Why is everyone so interested?"

"It's a big job you've taken on."

"So people keep telling us," said Dad. "But it's not as bad as you all seem to think. The last people did quite a lot of work on the roof and the woodwork. A lot of the big stuff's perfectly OK."

"Ah, the last people," said the man.

"Who were they?" asked Dad.

"I don't remember their names or anything

about them. I remember them coming round here, though, just like you, determined to make a go of it, going to make the place beautiful. Mind you, I don't doubt that it could be and I don't doubt that they meant to do it. But they'd hardly been there a month before they left. In a real hurry as well. Never came back. They put the house up for sale. Nobody came near it for years. They couldn't *give* it away."

"Well," said Dad. "I won't say it was given away to us."

"Perhaps not. But you didn't pay the earth for it, I'll be bound."

"But why did they go?" insisted Dad.

"I don't know. But I've got a pretty good idea. And I'll tell you this: there aren't many round here who'd spend a night in it, even for a bet. That place has got a bad reputation."

"For what?" William demanded.

"A hundred and twenty years old, that house is. Dyson built it himself, that I do know."

"So do we," said Dad. "There's a date and initials over the door."

"Well, there aren't any Dysons round here any more."

"Where did they go?" asked William.

"I don't know. But he didn't live in his own house very long, I can tell you that. And Dyson wasn't the only one who left it for ever."

The conversation had been overheard by another customer, a builder in boots and trousers stained yellow with sharp sand.

"You talking about Dyson?" he said. "I'll tell you what my old grandad always said. Dyson had the house built himself and then lived there with his sister Annie. He never got married: no woman in her right mind would have him. Surly devil he was. Liked the bottle too much. And Annie wasn't much better, though she was a hard worker: my grandad gave her that, at least. Not like her brother. Anyway, Dyson was drowned. A woodman found him in Marston Mere."

"That's the lake in the middle of the woods, isn't it?" said Dad. "I've heard of it."

"That's it. There aren't many would go *there* at night."

"Good fishing in it, though," said the man behind the counter.

"Annie was left on her own," said the builder. "But not for long. She'd gone completely dulally. She had to be shifted off to the asylum. Spent the rest of her life gabbling a lot of stuff no one ever understood."

"So that's the story of Dyson's Cottage," said Dad. "Not a very pleasant one. But I don't see why it should worry us."

"Ah, but there's something else my grandad used to say. Dyson and his sister weren't the only ones in the cottage. Once, there was an orphanage in Marston. And the warden wasn't above hiring some of the children out as cheap labour. My grandad said his father knew a woman living in the town who'd grown up in that orphanage. When she was eighteen and well out of it, she got married. She always said she had a sister once. That sister had been taken away by Dyson to skivvy for him. And that was the last anyone heard of her."

"Was it true?" asked Dad.

"Who knows? Nobody tried to find out. It was too late then – and besides, what did one orphan more or less matter? That's what they thought in 1880."

Rosy listened to all this without saying a word. She heard Dad asking all the questions as if nothing had happened – as if things were just the same as yesterday. But they weren't – and what the two men had said made strange thoughts she did not understand course through her mind.

"Well, thanks very much for telling us all that," said Dad. "It's nice to know our house has got a bit of history." His face said, *That's it, that's all we need to know. We're going now.* But Rosy did not want to leave yet. There was something she needed to ask.

"Did Dyson's Cottage ever have a well?" she asked.

"I don't doubt that it would, though I guess it would be filled in by now," said the builder. "Nobody was going to pipe water all the way out there just for one house in 1880 when the town was hardly on a mains supply yet."

"Same with the electricity," said the man behind the counter. "That wouldn't have come till much later."

Dad spoke sharply to Rosy.

"Stop wasting our time. You've got work to do." He indicated the heavy trolley. "You can push that for a start."

She leant to the handles of the trolley and started pushing. The two men watched them go.

"I'd rather you than me," the builder called out after them. "Nobody's lasted in that house. And nobody round here would try, for all it's been going for a song all these years. It's still got a bad reputation."

"The estate agent never told us any of this," said Dad.

"Well, he wouldn't, would he," replied the man.

Chapter 14

They drove home silently. The heavy trailer bumped ponderously behind them. The sky was dark grey, nearly black, when they reached the field and stopped outside the gate. Dad said, "You sit tight, Louise." He turned and looked straight at Rosy. "You open it," he said.

Rosy had had enough. She couldn't just submit to slavery.

"I've pushed the heavy trolley and I've done all the loading. Why can't the others do something for a change? It isn't fair."

"If you want to stay with us, you'll do as I tell you," said Dad. "If that means doing all the heavy work, then so be it. You're not family so you have no rights."

"But I *am* family. I've always been..." Rosy started. Then she saw again the row of stony faces in front of her. If she were going to have a big row about this, now was not the time, she thought. Ah, but if you do what he says now, you'll always be doing it, said another voice in her mind. She hesitated. And her nerve failed her. She got out of the car, felt a cold wind, knew that rain was not far away – and leant to the heavy gate.

As they crossed the field, the first drops of rain fell. Rosy presumed they would leave the trailer where it was, with everything snug under the waterproof cover. But Dad obviously thought otherwise. He stopped the car outside the cottage and then said to Rosy, "I want everything out of that trailer and stacked up *now*."

With that, he stalked out of the car, slamming the door behind him, and disappeared into the house. William and Louise, without even a look at Rosy, followed him.

Rosy sat still for a moment, unable to comprehend what was happening. After a minute, Dad appeared again in the doorway.

"Get on with it," he shouted.

When will *the time for argument come?* she thought. *Why is it never* now?

At least she had her waterproof anorak on. The rain was not at its hardest yet, but it was building up for a good downpour. She un-hooked the cover from the trailer, picked out the first armful of cable and sockets and pre-pared to run with it round to the back of the cottage where the outhouses were. Then she stared in horror. Dad must mean all those heavy bags of mortar and concrete as well. First – she wouldn't dare let them get wet. Second – she would have to get the wheel-barrow out to take them round.

She replaced the cover, carried the first lot of cable and sockets into the dry outhouse, brought the wheelbarrow out and stood it by the trailer. She was just about to take the cover off again when she realized Dad was watching her.

"You're just stupid with it, aren't you?" he said contemptuously. "Nobody but a fool would try to shift those bags with cement in them in the pouring rain. Do you want it set before we start? Just get yourself in here and wait until it's finished. I suppose we'll have to feed you even if you aren't worth it."

Rosy was suddenly aware of the lovely smell of a hotpot drifting out of the house. While they were away, Mum had made a good, hot, filling lunch. For her?

He disappeared inside again. Rosy leant against the side of the car in the pouring rain – and now tears mingled with the rainwater on her face. What was happening? Why was she being rejected? This was no game the rest of the family was playing. They *meant* it. Dislike and contempt showed in every movement, every glance, every word they spoke.

Why?

Then, clear as if spoken right beside her, came the voice again "...you cannot save me until you have suffered as I suffered ... there are more ghosts here ... strong ghosts who will fight you..."

The voice was gone. "Come back," Rosy whispered. "Tell me more." But she was alone again in the rain. Except for the smell of the hotpot. Yesterday it would have delighted her: today it mocked her.

She went indoors. She sat down at the table. William and Louise either side of her managed, even though the table was small, to shift away from her ever so slightly. Mum served Rosy last. She received a tiny portion with all the scraggy bits.

Lunch finished. Rosy had eaten slowly, looking at the others. They all ate quickly, silently, with second helpings which were denied her. But she wouldn't have wanted one even if it was offered: she was so unhappy she could hardly get down the gristly objects she was given to start with.

"You'll eat in another room in future," said Dad. "There's not enough space here for William and Louise."

Why? she wanted to say again, but couldn't. It was all of a piece with being made to do all the work. She reasoned again with herself. If she was being turned into a servant girl, her case would be stronger if she found out *exactly* what that was going to mean. *Rubbish*, said that other voice in her mind. *You're just scared of them all. And you know you've nowhere else to go.* It will change, said the first voice. They will see how wrong they are in the end. *Fat chance,* said the second voice. Besides, said the first voice, remember what I heard in the garden this morning? "*You cannot save me until you have suffered what I suffered.*" *And you believe that?* said the second voice.

"Yes, I do," said Rosy aloud.

When the plates were empty, Mum said to Rosy, "Stack them up on the draining board." No name, no "please". It was continuing the way it had started – and it wasn't just Dad. Then Mum smiled at William and Louise. "There's no need to help with the washing up and drying before the afternoon's work. She'll do it." Mum never looked at Rosy.

"And when you've finished that, there's all the unloading still to do," said Dad.

The rain had stopped by now. Rosy, without help, struggled with the concrete. She somehow manhandled the bags out of the trailer into the wheelbarrow and staggered round with it to another outhouse to stack them where they would be dry. The new wood followed. An hour passed before the trailer was empty and the outhouses full.

Dad stood over her as, gasping and weary, she finished. "The long grass has to go," he said. "You'll do it. Use the shears." He hardly looked at her as he spoke.

This was just unfair. "But it needs a big scythe. You said so yourself," Rosy burst out. "It will take days to do with a little pair of shears."

"Well, we haven't got a scythe, have we, you fool," said Dad. "So use the shears. And finish by supper. Or…"

William and Louise finished the sentence for him, mockingly. "*No food tonight.*"

Now Rosy could say it.

"Why are you doing this? Something's happened, hasn't it. I deserve to know what it is."

"Nothing's happened. You're not family. That's reason enough," said Dad icily.

That phrase again, as if it justified everything.

"You should thank God we took you in," said Mum. "Where would you be without us,

I wonder? So if we keep you, we want our money's-worth."

William laughed as he repeated Dad's words. "Not family, Rosy. Not family."

The long grass was wet. It only took Rosy a minute to realize the shears were very blunt. When she tried to cut the grass near the roots, it would not be sliced off. Instead, the long green blades just bent across the dull metal blades of the shears – and Rosy couldn't help it. She cried with sheer frustration. And her frustration was not just with the wet grass.

What had brought all this on? Of course she wasn't real family. She'd always known that. She'd been adopted. But she'd never been anything but family. She'd been shown off to the world as William and Louise's elder sister and had been as happy and wanted as they were. So why? Why?

"The ghosts ... they will fight you…"

The voice again.

She didn't care any more about what Dad said. She had to get out of this place. She threw the shears down and waded through the long grass to the fence at the side of the garden beyond which Marston Woods stood. To go in there, struggle through its dark, shaded reaches, never come out again…

She scrambled over the fence. Not one moment later, she was under the first trees of the ancient woodland, her feet squelchy in the leaf-mould of ages. The gloom, made lighter by the tracery of sunshine through the leaves as the sun struggled out overhead, was somehow soothing. She blundered on between gnarled trunks, the same words echoing through her mind. "Why? Because of the ghosts … they will fight you…"

She didn't realize she had found a path through the trees until she had been following it for some time. If there was a path, then she couldn't get lost. The thought disappointed her: she would like to stay in this cool, wet, quiet darkness for ever. She began to wonder why she had ever thought Marston Woods menacing.

The path met another one coming in from the left. And with it was something else. A stream which burbled and chuckled along as tree roots reached into the water along its banks. She realized she had heard the sound for some time without knowing what it was. A stream and two paths joined up: this was somehow disturbing. The lovely solitariness she had looked for in the woods was gone already. But she followed them, until she realized the stream was widening into a pool – and wider still. A small lake. A weak sun shone directly down on it. Round the shores were fishing platforms. So the paths she had found must be well used. But not, thankfully, today.

She stood on a tiny, pebbly shore looking out over the water. So this was Marston Mere.

What did she know about Marston Mere?

Of course. Dyson. "…he was found drowned. A woodman found him in Marston Mere."

She had come to the very place where the bad things of years ago had ended: Dyson dead here, sister gabbling gibberish in an asylum, a skivvy from the orphanage – someone else's sister – disappeared.

The puny sun gave up the struggle. Clouds

covered it. Rosy shivered. The water looked cold, deep, somehow thick, like an oil slick. And voices came again, right by her ear. "Finish by supper ... or no food tonight."

But the voices were not Dad's or William's or Louise's. What she heard was hard, strange, a man's. And she had heard it before. Where? In a dream?

She looked again at the forbidding water which had once closed over Dyson's head.

Then she turned and ran and did not stop until she reached the cottage fence. No matter where she went, she would not be alone. The ghosts would follow her: the ghosts would lie in wait for her.

She burst into the cottage. Dad, for all his forbidding of everybody else, was upstairs with Mum. He had taken floorboards up on the landing and was paying out electrical cable through holes he had drilled in the joists underneath.

Rosy didn't hesitate. She ran upstairs, remembering to miss the unsafe steps. She faced them as they carried on with their work, ignoring her.

"*Stop it!*" she shouted. "What you've been saying to me today and making me do, it isn't *you*! I'm not your slave and when you adopted me it wasn't so you could have one. I'm your *daughter*, as much as Louise is."

"Such insolence," said Mum, without looking up.

Dad stopped what he was doing for a moment. "You tried to escape this afternoon," he said. "Just get this into your head: you'll never leave here. So don't even try."

"*Why are you doing this to me?*" cried Rosy despairingly.

Dad stood up. "Why did we bother to take you on?" he said. He raised his arm as if to strike her.

Rosy couldn't help it. She turned tail and ran downstairs. As she went, she heard Dad's voice. "She hasn't touched that grass. We'll have to do something about this."

"Take her back?" asked Mum. "Get another one?"

She burst into the downstairs bedroom and threw herself sobbing on to her sleeping bag.

Chapter 15

Rosy was made to eat on her own at supper. She was pushed off into the old wash-house outside with bread scraped with margarine and an apple going rotten. A mug of tea was left for her: reboiled water had been poured over old teabags left in the teapot. The resulting liquid was weak, nasty and barely hot.

She ate and drank merely because she was hungry. This was not how life was to be from now on, surely? If it was – well, she hadn't been trying to escape for good that afternoon, whatever Dad thought. Perhaps, though, she should. But where? Who would believe, even *listen* to her? There would be no bruises on her: she was sure she would never be hit. No, she would be brought back. Mum, Dad and the children would seem so pleased at seeing her all the while the police or Social Services were in the house. Social workers would call her ungrateful and wicked – but once they were gone, it would be worse than ever. No, there was no escape.

So *why?* – that question she'd sought an answer for all day – was this happening?"

The ghosts ... they will fight you.

She would never get those words out of her head. And she thought again – of that lake in the woods with the oily, sinister water. And she knew what she had not realized then. She had not come back from there alone. Even as she had looked at the water and known Dyson had once been underneath it, other voices, a man's and a woman's seemed to speak, from far away.

"We're here, Rosy. We never left our cottage even when we were dead. And now we're in your family. You'll *never* escape us."

She had no idea how long she stayed alone in the old wash-house. By the time she stirred herself, it was dark and cold. That skivvy must have spent hours in here in Dyson's day, pounding clothes, forcing them through the mangle, probably eating in here as well. Rosy shivered at the thought and went outside. In the yard, she stood bathed in the light of Tilley lamps shining through the windows. The house looked cheerful and inviting – but closed to her now. She turned the handle of the back door, half-expecting it to be locked against her.

They were playing cards round the little table. Without looking up, Mum said, "Wash up your tea things, put them away and then get out of here."

Without saying a word, Rosy did so. When she had finished, she went to the bedroom, realized the Tilley lamp had been taken into the scullery, looked for her torch and switched it on.

Then she saw her own sleeping bag and airbed were gone.

Steps sounded through the doorway. Dad stood behind her. He spoke.

"You didn't think you'd be allowed to sleep

here with *our* children, did you? No, since William tells me you're so expert at climbing the stairs, you can go up there from now on. The little room at the end. That's yours from tonight."

This was too much. Tears clouded her eyes. Through her sobs, she managed to say, "This isn't fair."

Dad's voice was harsh. "What are you but a skivvy? For all we get out of you, we may as well not have bothered. Be thankful we're so generous. We could have let you starve."

Rosy turned and faced him. She saw his face, grim where the dark took over from the glow of the torch. And the thoughts which had obsessed her all day came back. Until yesterday, his had been a kind face, a generous, laughing face. He *was* her father. She wanted no other. But, well, yes, she *was* adopted. That was a fact of life: there was no use wishing otherwise. She was never jealous of William and Louise: they'd never been resentful of her. She was their sister and their parents were her parents. Who had ever questioned it?

So what had made this terrible change take place?

The anger and resolve Rosy knew she should have been feeling all day finally flooded into her. But she would not lose her temper.

"This is *wrong*," she said to him levelly. "I don't know why you are doing this, but it is *wrong*. If you didn't want me, you should never have taken me on. If you *do* want me, you shouldn't change. I *was* your daughter and I should *stay* your daughter."

Dad's face creased up with rage. "Get out of my sight," he roared. "Get up those stairs. I don't want to see or hear you until morning. You'll get your list of duties pushed under the door."

"I won't," she said, facing him.

Dad raised his arm. This time he really did seem about to hit her.

I won't let him betray himself into that, Rosy thought. She walked past him, head held high. He reached for her torch.

"Give me that," he grunted. "The light through the window's good enough for you."

She couldn't stop him grabbing it from her. Nevertheless, she looked coolly at him, then walked slowly and deliberately upstairs.

At the top, she stopped. Dad stood at the foot of the stairs, holding her torch, watching her. Mum stood beside him. William and Louise stood either side. They were both, Rosy noticed, sniggering.

It was strange. "*The ghosts ... they will fight you.*" All day she had assumed that only applied to her. But what if that wasn't true? What if Mum, Dad, William, Louise were being fought by the ghosts as well? There was evil in this house. What if only the evil had taken hold of them, so that what they were doing to her was the same as her half-known friend from long ago had gone through? Suddenly she was sure of it. The ghosts spoke to them as much as to her. But they had spoken in vastly different voices.

Now her feelings towards the family changed. All she felt was a sort of pity. How could she feel anger against people who could not help what they did? But that second voice in her mind that had told her to fight back remained unconvinced. How could she love people who had so completely and unreasonably turned against her?

She closed the door behind her. The air struck very cold. There was still a dusky light coming through the small window. But she caught again the musty smell and knew with a sudden certainty that she would be the first to sleep in this room for many, many years. In fact, since … *of course. This would have been the room of the orphan skivvy.*

She laid the airbed out and spread the sleeping bag on it. Her nightclothes must still be downstairs. Well, she wasn't going down there again. Besides, it was so cold in here – far too chilly for a nightie. So she merely took her shoes and socks off and slipped into the sleeping bag with jeans and top still on. Now she gave herself up to the silence of the room, without light, without life – *and without the everlasting whispering of the night which she had endured downstairs.* If those were ghosts, they were not up here.

Oddly, she felt good about herself. The

worm had finally turned. She had endured the day in a disbelieving dream, not knowing what was happening. But she had faced them, stood up to them in the end, even if Dad had taken her torch away. Yes, in spite of all that had happened that day, *she had won. They would not get to her. They would not have it their own way. She would be no skivvy.*

Skivvy? What an old-fashioned word. The lowest, most menial servant, who did all the rotten, dirty jobs. And today that word was all round her. The man in the builders' merchants, Dad, *she herself* – suddenly everybody seemed to be using it. And who were the skivvies? She was. So Dad said. And so was the girl Dyson had taken in from the orphanage and who had disappeared.

That must be what this was all about. For the first time Rosy had space, quiet and calm to think sensibly.

The ghosts ... they will fight you.

Were they fighting her through the rest of the family? Was that what her dreams were all about? Was this why Louise had been frightened the moment they came here, why

William kept saying the house didn't like him? Was this why nobody stayed? Did this happen every time to people who tried to live here?

At once, Rosy knew it did not – there were no dreams, no strange night companions, no sudden rejections of anybody. It was the atmosphere, the whispering, the presences which drove the other families out. What was happening here was to the five of them alone.

But *why*?

She thought over the story of the morning. Dyson and his sister. The girl from the orphanage. Unwanted, forgotten, disappearing and nobody bothered. Dyson, run away, drowning himself. His sister, mad, whom nobody could understand – or, more likely, nobody *tried* to understand. And now *she* was the skivvy – while Mum, Dad, William, Louise were like Dyson and his sister.

Had they all come here just for history to repeat itself? And if so, why them?

She remembered her dreams, the unseen presence who walked beside her, the soft voice which spoke to her, the sobs, the misery.

And the figure she had seen in the garden the morning before – just for a second. What had William said? "Have you got a twin we don't know about?"

Inklings of what it all meant were forming in her mind. They both frightened and satisfied her.

Too much thinking. Go to sleep.

She lay back on the raised pillow at the end of the airbed and closed her eyes. She was far more at peace now than she would have thought possible throughout today.

And now came that feeling again which had been there so strongly when they arrived, just when Louise had said, "Mummy, I'm frightened." Just once or twice it had come again, but now it took her as a complete conviction. *This is where we have to be. This is my place: this was meant for me.*

She did not know how long she slept. But now, as the moon and stars of a clear night shone through the window, she woke. The silence was so profound it was like thunder in her ears which was felt but not heard.

135

She was not alone in the room. A figure stood over her.

She saw the figure clearly, in far more bright detail than any moonlight ought to be able to give. She was looking at a girl of her own age. The girl wore a torn and dirty once-white smock. Her long hair was tousled. Rosy recognized her. She had seen her for so fleeting a moment the morning after her first dream.

Suddenly, she knew what William meant. She had not realized this in the garden, but now she saw. Apart from smock and hair, *she was looking at herself.*

The girl extended her hand.

"Come with me," she said.

"Who are you?" said Rosy.

"Rose, like you."

"Where are we going?"

"You'll see. The ghosts are fighting you. But this night you have gone far towards beating them. You have done what I could never do. You have faced them and they have not known what to do. But through doing that, you have found me at last. You will know who I am and why I am here. So now the final battle has come. That is what you came to Dyson's Cottage for."

Chapter 16

Rosy, without hesitation or fear, unzipped the side of her sleeping bag and stood up. She took the outstretched hand of the new Rose. Her bare feet expected the roughness of the floorboards: even at this strange moment, part of her mind worried about splinters. But there were none. Her feet seemed to be treading on something different. She looked down. She was walking on a worn rug she had never seen before.

The new Rose opened the door and led Rosy downstairs. There was a thin carpet on the landing and all the way down the stairs.

What had happened? She could make few details out in the moon's half-light. The strongest sensation was of sudden cold on her feet, of bare stones on the floor of the kitchen.

Her new companion spoke. "I am the Dysons' servant, their skivvy. I scrub this floor. I get up at four, I bring water from the well, I light the fires…"

"Yes," said Rosy. "I know." A vision of her own life, for ever more unless she broke free, stretched ahead. No fires, no well, but just as menial.

"This is the life of a skivvy." The voice of the new Rose was bitter. And Rosy realized something. Over a hundred years had passed – things were different now. *I could get out if I wanted to. It would be hard, but I could. I wouldn't have to be picked up by the police or Social Services like I thought this afternoon. There's opportunity for me. You never had that.*

Her feeling of happiness was dowsed in a second. *Where would I go?* Visions of railway stations at night, cold streets and shop doorways – and worse. Rosy gripped the hand of the new Rose hard. *You and I, after all these years – we are the same.*

They were outside now, in early morning

light. The new Rose had picked up a bucket in the scullery.

"This is my first job," she said. "We will go to the well."

William could not admit it, but he missed Rosy from the room. The whisperings in the night had been worse than ever. Louise had been badly frightened. She had whimpered for hours. At around midnight, the Tilley lamp's gas cylinder had run out. Suddenly, everything was down to him. He was the older, so the more responsible.

No, the stubborn voice inside him said. *You don't want her back. You can get along without rubbish like her. Pull yourself together.*

Oh, how he had tried. But the whispering never went away and it was two in the morning before he finally sank into a thin, fitful sleep.

He woke suddenly, to the same moonlight that Rosy had opened her eyes to. The whispering had gone. He listened to the silence.

Well, that wasn't so bad. We can get along on our own all right. Who needs her?

He felt quite pleased with himself. In the other sleeping bag, Louise now slept soundly. A new, wonderful day dawned in which he would watch someone else doing all the nasty work.

A noise outside the room. William stopped all his thoughts and listened. There it was again – a creak on the stairs.

He rose, stealthily crept to the door and opened it quietly.

He might have known it. Rosy, coming down the stairs with the twin she stubbornly refused to acknowledge. So that was it. Escaping. First this afternoon, now this early morning. Well, he'd put a stop to it.

He rushed over to Louise and shook her.

"Wake up, Louise. She's trying to escape again."

Louise woke. She didn't complain. She too tiptoed to the door. Together they watched the two figures – the one in front with long hair and smock, her follower in jeans and top.

"I bet she stayed dressed all night waiting for the time her friend was to come and get her," said William.

"We must tell Mummy and Daddy," said Louise. "She mustn't get away."

The garden presented a very different scene. It was as it had been in her dream. The path was new and weed-free: the bricks it was made of had hard squared-off edges. One side of the garden grew vegetables: the beans in rows climbing green and red up their long sticks, the darker green of peas, rows of cabbages – sprouts, savoys – still standing round and straight like fat soldiers, potatoes draped over their ridges. All of them growing out of dark, crumbly tilth without a weed daring to show its face. On the other side were the neat new chicken houses and runs from which satisfied clucks sounded. A red-combed cockerel was already preparing to crow.

At the far end were the neat, pruned blackcurrant and gooseberry bushes. Before they reached them, Rosy looked back. There stood the cottage, new slates gleaming, bricks new-pointed. Yes, this was what she had seen in her dreams and in those few seconds of vision the morning after the first one. Now she was really inside it – part of it, not just a visitor.

They walked forward together through the neat, low bushes. Here was the well. The new Rose slipped her bucket over the hook at the end of the rope, bent to the handle and turned it.

The sun was rising. Behind them came a re-sounding crow from the cockerel to welcome it.

The rope creaked downwards. Where it was coiled, the rope looked new. At the end where the hook was, where it was regularly doused in water, it was grey, frayed, rough. As the new Rose strained to turn it, Rosy could see how very thin her arms were.

William and Louise had slipped jerseys and shoes on. They had opened their parents' door, woken them up, endured their annoyance, watched while they pulled on coats and boots.

"So she learnt nothing this afternoon, I see," muttered Dad grimly. "She'll have to realize there's no getting away. This is her place and here she'll stay."

All four blundered through the kitchen and into the garden. Dawn streaked the sky. They could see clearly the length of the path and up to the bushes.

"They're in there. I know it," said Dad.

"But why go into the bushes if they're trying to escape?" said Mum.

"How should I know?" Dad replied testily. "Some piece of cunning to throw us off the scent probably."

He charged up the garden. The others followed. He plunged into the briars and thorns as if they didn't exist.

"But there's nothing inside," said Mum. "Just more bushes."

"Perhaps we'll see the well this time," said Louise.

Where the bushes were at their thickest and seemed to form an impenetrable wall, Dad had disappeared. But they heard his gasp of surprise – then his shout.

"Come on out. I know you're there."

With great difficulty they forced themselves through the worst of the barrier of briars. They heard him again: "Come on out. I know you're there."

Chapter 17

"*C*ome on out. I know you're there."
The man's voice came from just beyond the bushes. It was violent, harsh, slurred. Rosy had heard it before, in her dreams, on the morning of the vision. It frightened her.

The new Rose suddenly stopped crying. She froze. She looked up, listening. Rosy realized she was just a spectator now: she didn't exist any more for her new friend.

"*Come on out. I know you're there.*"

To Rosy, the words suggested strength and stupidity together. This man couldn't think of anything else to say.

And then he was there, in front of her, swaying, huge next to the tiled roof of the well and towering over the new Rose. He wore a collarless white shirt, breeches with both braces and a wide leather belt, big hobnailed boots. His face was red and unshaven. His eyes were bloodshot. Rosy knew he was very drunk. He blinked: this alone made her feel he had been out all night, had not slept and had rolled home with the dawn.

The new Rose looked at him transfixed, pale with sheer terror. It transmitted itself over the years straight to Rosy, whose stomach churned at the sight.

The new Rose faced the man. She let go of the handle. Her hands flew to her face as if to ward off blows.

With a noise that made Rosy jump, the handle started turning on its own. The rope unwound with a chattering whirr, which lasted no more than a few seconds. Then the bucket hit the water with a splash which echoed its way up the well shaft. The end of the rope parted from the turning handle and disappeared, making slapping noises against the sides of the shaft as it fell. Then came a second, more diffuse splash. The handle turned on its own, bare and useless, for a moment, then stopped.

Mum, Dad, William and Louise had pushed through the thick wall of bushes – and found it wasn't there. Nothing barred their way through.

"What *is* this?" shouted Dad.

"I told you there was a well, but nobody believed me," said Louise.

But they were all too intent on what lay in front of them to apologize to her. They could see Rosy – and with her the new Rose, both cowering in front of the large, nearly berserk man. Words indistinct through rage and drunkenness poured out of his mouth.

"Look at that. Fool. Now where's our water coming from? You're more trouble than you're worth."

He lunged towards the two Rosies. Mum suddenly called out to the man. "Go on. Sort them both out while you're at it."

Rosy did not move. She stood, scared but four-square with her new friend.

Dad shouted. "He's right. She can't be

trusted to do anything." He left his wife and children with a convulsive jump and stood by the swaying man, sharing the beer fumes which drifted through the morning air.

"*Come here!*" The drunk man lunged again. The new Rose gasped, backed away up against the well's brick surround. The man's grasping hands reached out, as if he would strangle her. The new Rose tried to scramble even further back. There was only one place to go. She sat on the rim and pulled her legs up so she was balancing on it entirely.

The man grasped for a third time. The new Rose teetered, terrified.

Suddenly, everything was very quiet. Rosy, Mum, Dad, William and Louise – all knew they were watching a scene from long ago, which could never change no matter how many times it was played out.

The man grabbed yet again. Did he make contact with her this time? None of them knew. The new Rose flinched yet again, tried to sway out of his reach, gave a strange little cry, then – as they all watched powerless – was gone.

They heard a scream and a splash. Then there was silence.

But the same thought coursed through all their minds. *Is that what we want for our Rosy? And not all of them said, "No!"*

Rosy, standing by the well's rim, saw the terrible new arrival. She heard his slurred words shouted right up next to her, felt his stinking breath, saw into his bloodshot eyes. The new Rose reached out her hand, touched her lightly on the sleeve. Rosy knew this little frightened gesture was for her alone: it meant goodbye. "Mr Dyson," she heard her whisper.

Then Dyson was closer still and moving forward. Did he touch her? Did the new Rose fall backwards and lose balance herself? No matter. As soon as Dyson moved, Rosy knew what would happen. When her new friend beside her disappeared, she knew such sorrow, such grief.

The family had watched what happened speechlessly. Even before scream and splash finally died away, Mum, Louise and William stepped back from the horror.

But Dad, next to Dyson, had his own words to shout. "See what happened to her? Well, it serves her right if she couldn't do what she's told. And you'll get the same." For the third time since yesterday morning he raised his hand as if to strike.

The echo had hardly died away and the spray from the splash dried on her face as she made herself look into the depths of the well, when Rosy knew the crisis was not over. She looked up – and there was Dad next to Dyson. His words, shouted loud not a metre away, were deafening. There was the same twisted, unreasonable anger on his face.

But Dyson had leant forward, both hands on the well's surround. He too was looking down, his face flecked with spray. His mouth was working.

As Dad raised his arm and brought it forward, Dyson's voice, anguished, horror-struck, cried out, a long wail. "N-O-O-O!"

Even before Dad's hand had descended, he

had turned, blundered past and knocked out of the way a woman in black long-sleeved dress and white apron who had silently arrived and stood fearfully just beyond the bushes. As Dyson ran down the path, boots thumping on the bricks, she stood watching him and her face was screwed up with terror.

Rosy saw her and recognized her in a split second. The woman in her first dream, who stood in the vegetable garden and sent silent messages of fear and warning. Dyson's sister.

But Dad was still close, arm raised. And now that arm was descending, fast but with seeming, horrible slowness, to make that blow he had been so close to twice already. But if this time he were to…? That well shaft was behind her.

She tried to move away, felt the bricks of the surround behind her, flinched further back – and found herself falling, falling, joining the new Rose…

She blinked. She was sitting, leaning up against a thick bush. Briars pierced her top and reached the skin on her back. Dad stood in front of her. Broken branches and leaves covered him.

Of Dyson and his sister there was no sign. Or the well. They were all wedged into what was not so much a clearing as a thinning of the bushes where Dad had done his cursory chopping down.

Dad's eyes were wide as he realized the truth. "If there *had* been a well there, I'd have sent you down it. Like *he* did."

Mum stood behind him. She looked dizzy, as if she had just been woken suddenly from a hideous dream.

"Rosy, what's happening?" she gasped. "Make it all right again, *please*!"

Rosy looked at the horrified, amazed faces of Mum and Dad and knew their shock was no less than her own. But somehow things had changed again completely.

"I don't understand," she said. "But I'm safe now. And so's Dad."

Dad turned round to her.

"No, I'm not," he roared. "Don't you see? I would have done the same. I'm as bad as him.

I deserve the same as him."

He pushed past them, knocking William and Louise aside as if they weren't there. He forced his way through the bushes. They heard his footsteps, just like Dyson's, on the remains of the brick path.

"But if he's as bad, then so are we," said Mum.

Rosy was sure then that her family had been possessed. She knew too who had possessed them – and that in those last few minutes it was in truth all over. But she didn't have time to bask in her sudden restoration to favour. "We've got to follow Dad," she said.

When they were outside the bushes, Dad was outside the garden. They saw in the long dewy grass where his feet had plunged. He had broken through the fence just where Rosy had crossed it yesterday when she ran into Marston Wood.

They followed. Rosy led the way. She somehow knew exactly where he would be going.

Once inside the boundary of trees, Rosy kept on. Mum and the children were behind her. "Where are we going?" panted Mum.

"He's never been in here. How does he know where he's bound for?"

"Don't you see?" Rosy looked back as she ran and shouted breathlessly. "It *is* all repeating itself. They're determined to win."

"Who?" cried Mum.

Rosy didn't answer. Dad's footprints in the leaf-mould were plain. Rosy knew they would soon meet the path she found yesterday which would in turn meet the second path which brought the stream. At length, they saw the waters of Marston Mere in front of them. As they reached its shores, a heron rose and flapped away over the trees.

"Where *is* he?" cried Mum.

Rosy, out of breath, pointed. He stood a hundred metres away, on a fishing platform, staring at the water.

Rosy ran with a last supreme effort, leaving the others behind. She knew what he was going to do.

"Dad," she called. "Don't let Dyson win. Come back."

He took no notice.

She reached the fishing platform, jumped

up on it, seized his hand. He tried to pull it away but she held firm.

"Dad, *listen* to me, please," she said. "This would be Dyson's victory after all. To make you do the same as he did, now we know his secret."

He turned a haggard face to her. "I tried to do the same. I'm no better than him. I deserve no more than him."

"No, Dad," Rosy said firmly. "You don't. He and his sister – the *bad* ghosts – they were strong. They fought us. They fought me through you. They *made* you reject me, as soon as Rose made herself known to me."

"You can never forgive me," said Dad.

"Yes, I can. It wasn't *you* who did that. It was Dyson and his sister. I know that now."

"That's not true," said Dad. "How can it be? I know what I thought."

"Dad, it *is* true."

"How can it be? What I tried to do to you is beyond forgiveness."

"It's not you I have to forgive," said Rosy. She saw his stubborn face. Dyson was still at work in him.

She spoke again. "But I tell you this, Dad. I *do* forgive you. Just as the other Rose, now it's all finished, forgives Dyson."

I have no right to say that, was the terrified thought that surged through her mind. *Yes, you have*, came another voice. *Because you're right. I do.*

Dad's hand, until now stiff with tension, began to relax. The others had reached the platform. "Come off there, *please*," cried Mum. There was fear in her voice.

"It's all over now," said Rosy.

Something seemed to crumple in Dad's face. He let go of Rosy's hand. It fell limply to his side. She took his arm. He allowed her to, and walked like a blind man as she guided him off the fishing platform.

The cottage with the sun making the slates shine blue and the windows flash looked cosy and inviting. When they first saw it as they left the woods, they knew that, after all, it would be a lovely home one day.

Dad's shoulders braced as he crossed the fence. When he entered the house, he said in the voice they all knew, "You're right. It's gone."

They came into the scullery. Rosy filled the kettle herself and lit the gas on the camping stove. It seemed to her fitting that she should. Soon they were all round the table drinking mugs of hot coffee.

"So there was something evil here," said Dad. "A violent man who persecuted his own servant girl and caused her death."

"And then drowned himself," said Mum. "Was that remorse, I wonder?"

"Or fear of punishment," said Dad.

"He might not have pushed her," said Rosy. "We don't know."

"Who'd have believed him?" said Dad. "We know he wasn't liked in the town. That made it worse."

"The two things together sent his sister mad," said Rosy. "I suppose she did her best to tell people but nobody listened."

"And they were all still here," said William. "The good ghost and the bad ghost. Rose and Dyson. And his sister. Waiting. The bad ghosts driving away the people they didn't want. Waiting for us."

"Why *us*?" said Louise.

"I think," said Rosy slowly, "it was because of me. Rose just *has* to be an ancestor of mine. She could only communicate with a blood relative. That's why Dyson had to take all of you over when he did. His secret in the well had to stay undiscovered."

Mum interrupted. "Rosy, can you ever forgive us?"

"Dyson was too strong for you all," she replied. "But Rose had to make her death known. She deserves a proper memorial. I came here to make amends."

"We must all make amends," said Dad.

Rosy was silent for a minute. The others waited until she spoke again.

"If Rose is related to me, I'm going to find out how."

Chapter 18

Summer ended, autumn passed, winter came. The house was gradually transformed. They spent a lovely Christmas together. Rosy, William and Louise all settled into new schools. After Christmas, Dad got a job in an engineering works on the industrial estate familiar to them because of the builders' merchants. Mum took a part-time job in a florist's.

By spring, the refurbishment of the house was pretty well complete. Outside, the relaid and resown lawn was showing green, the newly dug vegetable plot dark and weed free and awaiting its first seeds. The nature reserve Dad had promised Rosy on their first evening here burgeoned in a far corner.

At the other end of the garden were the bushes, pruned right down almost to the ground – perhaps even, one day, going to grow blackcurrants and gooseberries again. In the middle, the thickest bushes had been grubbed up to make a clearing. And, yes, there were traces of one-time brickwork here and rubble under the topsoil where something could have been filled in – by people who came later and who had no idea what they were covering when they arrived and the mains water arrived with them.

It was Rosy who had found this. Tears started at the back of her eyes when she made the discovery.

Her enquiries – in libraries, at the adoption agency, from old people who lived in the town – were beginning to get somewhere. The whole family pitched in to help. Mum and Dad had at last told her something about her parents. Before now, she had never really wanted to know. Now, the news that they were two students was like gold to her. She wrote to the college to ask if either had connections with Great Marston. And there were plenty of other ways of finding out. They all spent hours in libraries, looking at parish records, talking to old people in the town. Soon she would have real answers. Rosy would have traced the line between herself and the Rose who died.

There was only one job left. They had often talked about it. When they had decided, they found a stonemason in Great Marston.

And now, on a clear April evening, they stood together in the clearing in the bushes. Let into the ground, where the well once was, a carved stone lay.

IN LOVING MEMORY OF
ANOTHER ROSE

They stood, heads bowed, holding hands.

Then they went indoors, to their new home and their new lives.

Epilogue

*T*hank you so much. Now we can all rest in peace. My fate is known. So is his guilt.

You will never see us, never hear us again. The house is free at last, for ever. Enjoy it.

And I shall always be here, with you, sharing, watching.

≡IPPO GHOST

Summer Visitors

Emma thinks she's in for a really boring summer,
until she meets the Carstairs family on the beach.
But there's something very *strange* about her
new friends. . .
Carol Barton

Ghostly Music

Beth loves her piano lessons. So why have they
started to make her *ill*. . . ?
Richard Brown

A Patchwork of Ghosts

Who is the evil-looking ghost tormenting Lizzie,
and why does he want to hurt her...?
Angela Bull

The Ghosts who Waited

Everything's changed since Rosy and her family
moved house. Why has everyone suddenly
turned against her. . .?
Dennis Hamley

The Railway Phantoms

Rachel has visions. She dreams of two children
in strange, disintegrating clothes. And it seems
as if they are trying to contact her...
Dennis Hamley

The Haunting of Gull Cottage

Unless Kezzie and James can find what really
happened in Gull Cottage that terrible night
many years ago, the haunting may never stop...
Tessa Krailing

The Hidden Tomb

Can Kate unlock the mystery of the curse
on Middleton Hall, before it destroys the
Mason family...?
Jenny Oldfield

The House at the End of Ferry Road

The house at the end of Ferry Road has just
been built. So it can't be haunted, can it...?
Martin Oliver

Beware! This House is Haunted
This House is Haunted Too!

Jessica doesn't believe in ghosts. So who *is*
writing the strange, spooky messages?
Lance Salway

The Children Next Door

Laura longs to make friends with the children
next door. But they're not quite what they seem. . .
Jean Ure

HIPPO ANIMAL

Have you ever longed for a puppy to love, or a horse of your own? Have you ever wondered what it would be like to make friends with a wild animal? If so, then you're sure to fall in love with these fantastic titles from Hippo Animal!

Thunderfoot

Deborah van der Beek

When Mel finds the enormous, neglected horse Thunderfoot, she doesn't know it will change her life for ever…

Vanilla Fudge

Deborah van der Beek

When Lizzie and Hannah fall in love with the same dog, neither of them will give up without a fight…

A Foxcub Named Freedom

Brenda Jobling

An injured vixen nudges her young son away from her. She can sense danger and cares nothing for herself – only for her son's freedom…

Goose on the Run
Brenda Jobling

It's an unusual pet – an injured Canada goose.
But soon Josh can't imagine being without him.
And the goose won't let *anyone* take him away
from Josh. . .

Pirate the Seal
Brenda Jobling

Ryan's always been lonely – but then he meets
Pirate and at last he has a real friend...

Animal Rescue
Bette Paul

Can Tessa help save the badgers of Delves Wood
from destruction?

Take Six Puppies
Bette Paul

Anna knows she shouldn't get attached to the
six new puppies at the Millington Farm Dog
Sanctuary, but surely it can't hurt to get just a
little bit fond of them...

Goosebumps

R.L. Stine

Reader beware, you're in for a scare!

These terrifying tales will send shivers up your spine:

Goosebumps